# THE GIRL,

# THE DRAGON,

# AND THE WILD MAGIC

# THE GIRL, THE DRAGON, AND THE WILD MAGIC

Book One of The Rhianna Chronicles

Dave Luckett

## SCHOLASTIC INC.

New York   Toronto   London   Auckland   Sydney
Mexico City   New Delhi   Hong Kong   Buenos Aires

ISBN 0-439-41187-4

Text copyright © 2000 by Dave Luckett.

Originally published in Australia in 2000 by Omnibus Books under the title *Rhianna and the Wild Magic*.
All rights reserved. Published by Scholastic Inc., 557 Broadway, New York, NY 10012, by arrangement with Omnibus Books, an imprint of Scholastic Australia.

SCHOLASTIC and associated logos are trademarks and/or registered trademarks of Scholastic Inc.

12 11 10 9 8 7 6 5                    4 5 6 7 8/0
                                              40

Printed in the U.S.A.
First American edition, October 2003

To the real Rhian,
who has her own magic

# CHAPTER 1

"Think, Rhianna." Mrs. Greenapple leaned over the front of Rhianna Wildwood's desk and pointed to the words in the spellbook. "It's just a simple rhyme to say over a sleeping potion. Now repeat after me, *Doremus dorema doremasa sleepy soppy dormousey casa. . . .*"

The class at the Smallhaven village school was quiet except for the turning of pages, but Rhianna knew that everyone was looking at her. She frowned and tried again: *"Doremus dorema doremasa, sleepy soapy . . ."*

*"Soppy,* Rhianna."

Rory Spellwright, two seats to the right, sniggered and whispered something to his friend Fion Oldbuck. Rhianna felt her chest grow tight. She hated giving Rory something to use against her, but it was so hard to get spellcasting right. None of the words made any sense.

*"Soppy . . .* what does that mean, Miss?" she asked.

Rory sniggered again.

"Never mind what it means, Rhianna, just say it." Mrs. Greenapple was a little impatient this morning, and her voice showed it.

"Yes, Rhianna, just *say* it, stupid," mimicked Rory, so low that Mrs. Greenapple didn't quite hear him.

"What was that, Rory?" she asked.

"Nothing, Miss," said Rory, virtuously. "Just going over the chant in my book."

Mrs. Greenapple nodded, and bent over Rhianna's desk again.

Rhianna hated being singled out like this. *"Doremus dorema doremasa, sleepy soppy enormously . . ."*

*"Dormousey,* Rhianna — oh, no! Stop! I didn't mean that!"

Too late. There was a sudden thump. Rhianna swung around in her seat, and there was Tom Bodger, slumped forward over his desk. The thump had been his head hitting it. He was fast asleep, snoring like a bulldog pup.

Mrs. Greenapple pressed a hand to her mouth. Then she glared at Rhianna. "Now look what you did," she said crossly.

"Me?" asked Rhianna.

"Yes, you." The teacher shook Tom's shoulder. He stayed asleep, snoring a little. "You said 'enormously.' You must have increased the power of the spell." She put her hand on Tom's head and said something in a whisper. It made no difference. Tom was sound asleep.

"But *you* said the next word, the one that —" started Rhianna.

Mrs. Greenapple cut her off. "Never mind what I said. Just help me wake Tom up."

*Just like always,* Rhianna thought. *First they tell you to listen to everything they say, and then they tell you not to. It isn't fair.*

Rory put on an expression of great concern. "Miss," he called, "has she killed Tom? Should I get my uncle?"

Rory's uncle was the nearest thing the village had to a real wizard. Mr. Spellwright had a spell shop, just down the street.

"No need, thank you, Rory," said Mrs. Greenapple, hauling Tom upright. "He's just asleep."

But Tom wouldn't wake up, not right away. They had to carry him out and put his head under the pump, and all he did at first was blow happy little bubbles. It took twenty minutes and two buckets of water to wake him up enough for him to go home.

The class giggled. Mrs. Greenapple fumed. "The magic shouldn't have gone *that* wrong," she said. The school's spell wards must have run down again. Still, the lesson had been ruined, and it was all Rhianna's fault.

Rhianna sighed. *It was always the same,* she thought.

But there was worse to come before lunch.

"Wands down. Look at me. No talking." Mrs. Greenapple took up a pile of papers. "Here are your results from last week's test of Spell Ingredients. Quite good, and I'm pleased. Mostly." She began to send the papers skimming through the air, using a fly-and-find spell. Each one landed neatly on the right desk, and the fly part of the spell was turned off by each student with a flick of the fingers. "Ariadne . . . Gloriana . . . Ingold . . . Isembard . . . Fion — much better this week, Fion . . . oh, and Rhianna."

Rhianna's paper landed in front of her. She saw the big red marks on it and almost forgot to turn off the spell. When she did remember to flick her fingers, the piece of paper fell off the desk. It crashed to the floor like a sheet of metal, making a noise that echoed around the classroom. Everyone turned and stared.

Rhianna turned scarlet. Mrs. Greenapple took off her glasses and pinched the bridge of her nose, as if she had a headache. "I think you had better see me afterwards, Rhianna," she said.

Rhianna picked up the paper and looked at it. If anything, this test seemed worse than the last one. And she *had* studied for it, she really had. She peeked at the total, just lifting a corner of the paper off the desk, so no one else would see it.

Oh, no! F! Even worse than the D-minus she'd got for Recitation last week. And Spell Ingredients was her best subject, too. That was because it had measures and numbers in it, and they made sense. Not like spells.

Rhianna sat in silent dismay as her teacher called out the names of all the rest of the class, one by one. The dismay was made worse when nobody else was told to wait behind.

The bell rang for lunchtime as Mrs. Greenapple finished handing out the papers. "Look at your marks later. And talk about them outside, *if* you please, Morgana Hedger. Books away. Make sure your wands are properly laid east–west. Who's ready to go?"

Rhianna was ready to go, all right, but there was no chance of being able to get away. Mrs. Greenapple dismissed the class, row by row, line by line, making sure that Rhianna was among the last. There was no way to sneak out past her. She hadn't forgotten.

Rhianna waited, standing by her desk. Her friend Rose Treesong gave her a concerned look as she left the classroom, but Rhianna was too sunk in gloom to notice. The door closed, the sounds of play were hushed, and the bright sunlight outside made the room seem darker still.

"Well, Rhianna." Mrs. Greenapple folded her arms and leaned against her desk. "What's to be done? It seems you didn't take in a thing I said all last week. Or anything in the book, either."

Rhianna stared at the floor and said nothing.

Her teacher sighed. "I must admit, I can't understand it. Your work is neat and clear. You understand all the amounts . . . look, three-and-a-half scruples of butterfly-wing dust plus three quarters of a drachm of thistledown sap makes just about a pinch. . . ."

"It makes exactly a pinch!" Rhianna was stung. The table showing the amounts had been clear in the book. Difficult, mind you. She wished all the measures could go evenly into each other, but all the same. . . . She looked up. Mrs. Greenapple was shaking her head.

"How many times must we go over this, Rhianna?" she asked. "There is no such thing as 'exactly a pinch.' Nothing is exact in magic! Everyone's pinch is different. Far more important than the pinch is what it's a pinch *of*. That's what you were asked about. This is the base for a simple flying ointment. And what did you say it was? 'One pinch of gray goo.' Really!"

"Well, that's what it looked like," muttered Rhianna.

Mrs. Greenapple's face became grim. "Since when," she asked carefully, "has anything ever been what it looks like in magic?"

Rhianna looked down again. There was something about that question that set her teeth on edge. Why shouldn't things be what they looked like? Why should everything be vague and fuzzy and not exact?

But it was no use scowling. Mrs. Greenapple shook her head again. "Well," she said, "I think we need to talk to your parents, Rhianna. I wouldn't mind so much if you just forgot things. Still less if you just got a few of the words wrong or left out a gesture when working a spell. But this is far worse. It's as if you had everything around the wrong way, as if you . . . as if you didn't think magic was *real*. As if you thought there was some other way to make things work." She watched Rhianna's face, what she could see of it. When nothing more happened after a few moments, she sighed. "All right, Rhianna. I don't think there is anything more to be said now. I'll be sending a letter home. Go and have your lunch."

Rhianna trudged out, still scowling.

Rose was waiting for her in their usual place. Rhianna plumped herself down and opened her lunch basket.

"How bad was it?" asked Rose.

"The usual," said Rhianna, trying to look unconcerned. "You know, *'Rhianna, you have to remember that nothing is what it seems to be. Nothing adds up. Nothing is right.'* Why can't things say what they mean, and mean what they say?"

"Well," said Rose, considering, "I suppose it's because they don't in magic."

"Don't *you* start."

"I'm not starting. You asked me, I told you."

This was so true that Rhianna had nothing to say to it. Her pie was suddenly tasteless, though it was kept fresh by her mother's own spell. She dropped it back in her basket.

Mrs. Greenapple would be writing that letter already, and the sending spell would have it at Rhianna's house by this afternoon. She would have to face her mother and father over dinner.

That was enough to cause any amount of gloom. She'd be sent to her room after school every day for a week, most likely. Told to study. Study! As if it ever made any difference whether she studied or not! The things in the books didn't make any sense at all. Why should a finding charm work if you walked around a circle one way, but not if you walked around it the other? Why? Rhianna always wanted to know *why*. Mrs. Greenapple was always telling her it didn't matter why. *Just do it, Rhianna.*

"Just do it, Rhianna," she said out loud, and there was a rude laugh just behind her. Rory Spellwright's laugh.

It was Rory, all right. "Yeah, just *do* it, Rhianna. Why can't you? What's wrong with you? *I* can do it. All the other kids can do it, even the little ones. Even Rose here can do it, and she's nearly as dumb as —"

Rose whipped her head around, her eyes sparkling dangerously. She whispered a find spell and tossed a squashberry in the air. Up it went, gently, and then it curved in flight as if it had wings, flew faster and faster, and went *splat!* right in the middle of Rory's forehead. Purple juice trickled into his eyes, and he touched his fingers to his face in disbelief.

"Dumb, am I?" asked Rose. "Well, I've got a mean find spell and a basket full of squashberries. Get out of here, Rory, or you'll be so purple you'll think you're a grape."

Rory looked down at his purple fingers. His mouth opened and closed. "You wait," he raged. "You wait. I'll tell. I'll tell Mrs. Greenapple," and he ran towards the school building, his voice working up into a howl as he went.

Rhianna sighed. "You shouldn't have done that," she said. "He'll do it, for sure."

Rose nodded. "It'll be worth it," she said comfortably. "I should have used the whole bunch on him."

"Waste of good squashberries," said Rhianna. She sighed again. "Why does he have to be such a sneak?"

Rose shrugged. "Could be because he doesn't have much power, no matter how right he gets the spell, and he hates that. He couldn't have done that with the squashberry, for instance. Could be because nobody takes any notice of him unless he's acting like he does. But the main reason is just Rory. He just likes himself that way, I suppose." She glanced across the meadow. "Here we go."

Mrs. Greenapple was coming towards them. Rory walked behind her, looking woeful when she glanced at him, and poking his tongue out the rest of the time.

"I'll probably be kept in," said Rose. "You'll have to walk home by yourself."

Rhianna nodded. It was so unfair.

When school was over, Rhianna slouched up the village street towards home. The worst of it was that she had to stop at Mr. Spellwright's shop. Her mother had asked her to pick up some amber for a preserving spell.

Mr. Spellwright was standing at the shop door, his thumbs in his waistcoat pockets. Rhianna's mother had always told her to be very polite to Mr. Spellwright because he was an important man, and well-off, and had the only spell shop in the village. He was tall and portly, with a long face like a hound's, but his eyes were a lizard's eyes, sharp and glittery.

"Good day, Mr. Spellwright," said Rhianna.

Mr. Spellwright looked straight through her and sniffed. His thumbs remained in his waistcoat pockets. Mr. Spellwright didn't like people who were new to the village, like the Wildwoods. And he liked to think of himself as a wizard and a person far superior to Rhianna's father, who was the village blacksmith.

"I need to get ten grains of amber for Mother," Rhianna went on.

Mr. Spellwright grunted and turned his back, retreating into the darkness of the little shop. Rhianna followed him in.

It was darker and cooler inside, with odd shadows in the corners. They formed shapes that melted when you looked straight at them, but came back when you looked away. Magical ingredients of all sorts were stacked in rows on shelves, or filled big glass jars. Many of them looked or smelled odd — sharp or pungent or spicy or musky.

All sorts of strange ingredients were needed for spellcasting. Alum and peat, to make spells of shrinking and drying, for the clothmakers. Mermaids' purses, to make spells to call fish, for the fisherfolk. Lodestone and pelligorny, to make spells to find or hold, soapwort and rue and balsam, to repair or clean. Spells to make things grow, spells to work small changes, and spells to preserve, all with their own ingredients. Most people used some magic every day, and Mr. Spellwright supplied all the things they needed. He had a good business. It seemed that people needed more and more magic.

But that wasn't all there was in the shop. There were oddly shaped dusty glass bottles that never seemed to be used. There were pigeonhole racks at the back of the shop with small colored jars and even smaller vials that were never opened. It was difficult to see what was in them. People said that they contained weirder things yet, ingredients for greater spells than most folk could manage. Spells that needed the bones of strange animals, or leaves of the deadly upas tree, or even troll hide and dragon blood, serpent venom and elf-shot. There was a preserved snake floating in clear liquid in a large jar. Rhianna could never make out its tail. Both ends seemed to have heads — or were there two snakes? The colors of the scales seemed to come and go as she watched, and she thought the little black eyes followed her.

Mr. Spellwright slid behind his counter and took down a jar of amber dust from a shelf. He weighed out ten grains of it, poured it into a small paper bag, twisted the bag shut, and put it on the counter. Without saying anything, he held out a hand.

Rhianna gave him a coin. She picked up the bag and said, "Thank you, Mr. Spellwright," then turned and walked out of the shop, feeling his eyes on her back all the way. To reach the sunshine outside was a relief.

She trailed on up the street towards home. It wasn't a

long enough walk, between the little houses and beyond the village green, but she made it last as long as she could. That note from Mrs. Greenapple would have beaten her home. What on earth was she going to say to her mother?

# CHAPTER 2

Going home was every bit as bad as Rhianna had feared it would be.

She slipped in the back door, hoping to tiptoe through to her room and not come out before dinnertime. Her mother's back was turned to her as she peeled potatoes at the bench. Rhianna moved very quietly, but she wasn't quiet enough. Meg Wildwood looked around.

"Ah, there you are, Rhianna," she said. "Late back from school, I see."

*Oh dear,* thought Rhianna. She smiled. "Yes, Mother. I thought I'd go straight through and get started on my homework."

"Good, good," said her mother, nodding. "That's good, Rhianna. In fact, I think you need to do a lot more of that. You know about the note your teacher sent home, then?" She fixed Rhianna with a considering eye. "Of course you do." She pulled a piece of brownish paper from her pocket. "It says that you failed another test to-day. Mrs. Greenapple thinks you will have to repeat this year's work."

Rhianna stared at the floor.

Her mother looked at the note and frowned. "At least, I think that's what she wrote. I must say, the school really should use better spellpaper. This is falling to pieces already. But" — she put it back in her pocket — "I suppose your father will still be able to read it when he comes home."

Worse and worse.

"Mother . . . I tried. I studied, I really did. But it all gets mixed-up, somehow. It all comes out wrong. I get confused. There are no rules . . . nothing ever makes sense."

Meg shook her head. "Rules? Of course there are no rules. Human beings make rules, not magic. Magic is wild. At its heart, it's not to be tamed. We can only use it because there are ways of handling it that the great wizards work out by trial and error. You have to *remember* those ways. Or you'll never be able to use magic at all."

"Maybe I don't want to use it," mumbled Rhianna. "Father doesn't, much."

Meg's eyebrows went up. "Your father is a smith. There's nothing wrong with being a smith, Rhianna, but it's hard work, and magic isn't much help, with all that cold iron. We wanted something better for you. That's one of the reasons we moved out here from Avalon. Home Island was getting crowded. There's more magic in the country, with fewer folk to use it up. But there's no use in that if you won't learn the spells."

Rhianna shrugged. "Not won't. Can't."

Meg was silent for a moment. Then: "All right, Rhianna. I know you try hard, and it's true that magic isn't easy, not for everyone. Go and do your homework now, and try to remember what you read. I want to hear the chants as you go over them. We'll talk it over at dinner with your father. I'm sure it's not as bad as all that."

Rhianna went to her room, miserably. She sat at her table, opened her spellbook, and tried to learn the spell for that day. It said: *To freshen cut flowers — a pinch of rich earth and the words* Floribunda in abunda floribus *said twice with a pass of the hands, fingers spread, see diagram.*

She looked at the diagram. It was simple enough, and the spell didn't look too hard. There was a bunch of spring wildflowers in a jar of water on her windowsill, and some earth in a window box. She sprinkled the earth over the flowers, made the pass with her hands, and whispered the spell.

Nothing happened. Rhianna waited, disappointment growing. Sometimes, nothing happened. Sometimes . . .

Then the flowers — little spring flowers, pinks and

sunroses and cat's-eyes, bluebells and ladylocks and fairy bonnets — shook themselves. There was a soft tinkle, and the air swirled in strange colors. The flowers raised their heads. They straightened. Then they began to grow. Their stems grew long and strong and leafy, emerald green. And the flowers —

The pinks flushed deep crimson, red as a dragon's heart. Sunroses grew to puffs of bright shining gold the size of Rhianna's hand, their petals stiff as lace and edged with golden sparkles. Cat's-eyes blazed in stripes like candy sticks, shiny like satin. Rhianna watched, fascinated, as the ladylocks became knots of pearl ribbon with silver edges. They brightened until they began to twinkle like stars, tiny points of many-colored fire coming and going at their centers.

It was like . . . like growing your own jewel box. Rhianna stretched out a finger, wondering . . . *Did I do this?*

And as she touched, as her finger stroked the first bloom, suddenly it crumpled, the gorgeous colors faded, and it turned brown and then black. One by one, then all together, the flowers drooped and shriveled, and the dry leaves pattered to the floor, and the stems died back. A minute later, there was nothing but a bunch of dry sticks in a jar of water.

Looking at the ruined flowers, Rhianna began to cry. *I do nothing but make things worse,* she thought. *What use is magic like that?* She sniffled and wiped her nose with her hand. *And it's no use talking to Father about it. He won't understand.*

But when her father came home, late and tired, there was no talk about Rhianna's schoolwork.

Loys Wildwood was a big man, as big and strong as a smith should be, and he was usually easygoing, gentle as large people often are, and smiling. But now he looked thoroughly upset.

Dinner was laid on the table. Meg had given up waiting, and had called Rhianna from her room. The chants and the spell ingredients and the tables of herbs were already blurring in Rhianna's mind, though she had spent *hours* saying them over and over. They lay like cold wet stones in her head, heavy and slippery.

It worried her, but her father's face worried her far more.

"What's the matter, Loys?" Her mother's voice showed the same worry.

He tried to smile. "Oh, nothing. Just a problem at work."

"What sort of problem?" Meg Wildwood was a hard woman to shake off. Everyone said so.

"Just the new fire ward. It . . . won't work."

Rhianna knew what a fire ward was. It was a spell to

stop fires. Her father needed one, because the smithy had a fire going all the time, and there were houses all around. An accident might mean a bad fire.

Meg dished up peas. "I didn't know you needed a new one. Didn't you renew it just last month?" she asked.

Loys nodded. "Yes, I did. And it's failed already. I got Spellwright in to make it again, and he said he couldn't get it to work. He thinks the spot where I built the smithy is cursed. There's no magic there to make the spell, he said. It won't work, anyway."

Meg put down her spoon. "Won't work? That's not right. Spells have to work. If you make them properly, that is. Perhaps you —"

Loys shook his head. "Look, all I can tell you is what Spellwright told me. I'm no magician. He said there's no magic in that spot, and if I want the smithy insured against fire, I'll have to move it. I can't afford to move it, and I can't afford the risk of not having a fire-ward spell. I don't know what to do about it."

No magic there at all? Rhianna stared at her parents. Loys looked at his plate, glum and silent, and Meg watched him in turn, for what seemed like a long time.

Then Meg seemed to shake herself. She dipped into her pocket and pulled out the letter. The paper tore across as she brought it out.

Loys glanced at it. "What's that?" he asked.

"It is . . . well, it used to be . . . a letter from Mrs. Greenapple. Saying that Rhianna is doing very badly at school, and warning . . ."

Loys took the paper from her. He held it in two fingers, and it tore under its own weight. "It came home like this?" he asked. "Brown, tatty, falling apart?"

"Yes. Strange, isn't it? As if the writing spell was . . . was . . ."

"Failing." They sat in silence around the table, and the silence echoed back at them.

Then Loys nodded, as if to himself. "Spellwright says he's asked for a wizard to come out from the Queen's own court. All the way from Avalon. Something has to be done, he says. Too many spells have failed lately. It doesn't bother me much, except for this fire ward, but everyone else is suffering."

That was all he said for the rest of dinner. Afterward, Rhianna excused herself and went back to her room to work on her books again. It was just as it had been before. The spells skittered around in her head like a flock of chickens, hard to tell apart, always just a little out of reach, struggling and wriggling even when she caught one.

At bedtime her mother came in to say good night, as usual. A little line came and went on her forehead, smoothing out when she thought of it, returning after a moment.

"Time for bed, Rhianna," she said. "You've done as much as you can tonight."

Rhianna got up and washed her hands and face in the basin. She put on her nightgown.

"Mother?" she asked.

"Yes?"

"Do you think I'll have to do the year's work all over again?"

Meg sighed. "I don't know, Rhianna. I can't think just now. Go and say good night to your father."

So Rhianna padded out, kissed her father good night, and went to bed. But not to sleep, not at once. She kept saying the spells and the chants and the lists of spell ingredients over and over to herself, in the hope that they'd stick, but in between them came the worried look on her father's face and what he had said at dinner: *Too many spells have failed lately.*

Including all of Rhianna's spells. Maybe it wasn't all her fault, then. Maybe the magic itself was at fault. Or just the magic hereabouts. Maybe magic itself was the wrong thing to do. Well, it certainly didn't make people better, or any easier to like. Think of Mr. Spellwright. And Rory.

Or maybe it was just the wrong thing for her. After

all, she might not be suited to using magic at all. Like Father. He was a smith, and a good one. Using cold iron all the time meant that he could not weave spells, not even the little ones that most people used, because cold iron and magic were sort of opposites that canceled each other out. Maybe she could become a lady blacksmith.

She fell asleep thinking about that.

# CHAPTER 3

The next morning, Rhianna lined up outside her classroom with the others. She hadn't slept well. Her dreams
had been about things running away and getting less and
less. Sand running out of hourglasses; water leaking away
from dams. And it was Wednesday, and that meant Conjuration, first thing. Rhianna hated Conjuration. It was
worse than all her other subjects. The hand movements
had to be done just right, depending on the phase of the
moon and when your birthday was and whether your
hair was light or dark and all sorts of other silly things she
could never remember.

So she didn't notice anything when they went in, and
only looked around when she heard the class murmur.
Then she saw it. Mrs. Greenapple had washed the spellboard. Mrs. Greenapple only washed the board just before the holidays, or if someone important was visiting
the school. And it was still the middle of the term.

But the spellboard was washed and the floor had been swept and polished. More than that, Mrs. Greenapple seemed different. She had to start the opening invocation again, because she said the words the wrong way round the first time. She was wearing her best cape, too, the one she only wore to the opening of term and Parents' Night.

There was no Conjuration period, either, not straight away. Instead, Mrs. Greenapple took a firm grasp on her wand, waited until the class had settled, and then spoke: "Make sure your desks and chairs are neat, please. If there are any class library books, please put them back on the shelves now."

"Miss, I haven't finished reading mine." That was Merry Gladbetook, who read everything and remembered it all, like a sponge soaking up water.

"Nobody has finished, Merry. But I want the books all neatly put away. The school has a very important visitor this morning."

So that was what it was all about. Rhianna tidied her desk. At least it meant they wouldn't have so long for Conjuration.

When they had finished tidying up, Mrs. Greenapple looked at the sundial on the wall outside, across the courtyard. "All right," she called. "We'll start Conjuration, just to show our visitor what we can do, if he arrives. Get out your wands and spellbooks and turn to page fifty-three. The heading is 'Simple fire ward.' Quickly, now."

Despite herself, Rhianna felt a stir of interest. She turned the pages of her spellbook. A fire ward. That was the same sort of spell as the one that Father had had trouble with. Perhaps she could see what was wrong with it. She might even be able to help him.

She found the place and raised her head. Mrs. Greenapple was starting the first series of gestures. "Palms together, like this, fingers pointing upwards. Now, keeping your hands joined at the base, flutter your fingers for four beats."

Rhianna watched much more closely than usual and followed Mrs. Greenapple with care. A flicker of the fingers to show the fire, and then a soothing, broad sweep of the arms to show it being snuffed out. Fanning the face to invoke the heat of the flames, and hands across the eyes to show the sharp, burning glow. Now, water signs: fingers twitching, hands falling to show rain. A rolling of the arms and shoulders to invoke the waves of the sea. Rhianna watched Mrs. Greenapple's hands and did everything she did, making sure the water gestures were stronger than the fire gestures, so that the fire would be put out. Perhaps she should make them a little stronger still, to be perfectly sure. . . .

She was concentrating hard, trying to get it all exactly right, just this once. Concentrating so hard that she didn't hear Rose's yelp of surprise. She didn't even feel the first drops of rain.

It wasn't until she heard the first little clap of thunder that she realized something was amiss. There was a *phut!* sound, like a bag of sand being dropped on a floor. Then a sharp spark of lightning.

The other children were edging away from her and pointing. Mrs. Greenapple had stopped conjuring and was staring at her. Or rather, she was staring at a place above Rhianna's head.

Rhianna looked up.

A cloud was floating between her and the ceiling. It was small but inky, like a mass of black cotton wool. As Rhianna watched, it grew even darker and expanded like a balloon being blown up. It spat a sudden fork of lightning, thin as a thread, but blue-white and dazzling. Another crackle of miniature thunder sounded. It began to rain harder.

And there was something on the floor, something clear and wobbly like a jelly, and it was coming towards her, leaving a trail of water that soaked into the floorboards. It rolled like a great big drop of water, but it was getting bigger and bigger, gathering itself from some place that Rhianna couldn't see. The rain from the cloud fell on it, and on her. She realized that she was soaked to the skin.

Mrs. Greenapple found her voice. "Out! Everyone out!" she cried. "Open the door!"

The door slammed open. The nearest children tumbled out, and the others followed, while Mrs. Greenapple waved her arms in drying gestures. She started a drying spell: *"Desicca inati evapo summa . . ."*

But the words took no hold. The bubble of water, clear as glass, slid up to Rhianna and rubbed itself against her like a cat, growing larger all the time. Rhianna couldn't move. She knew she ought to do something about this, and she knew, in some dark place in her mind, that this was all her fault, but she stood numb with surprise and dumb with amazement.

Then a shadow fell across her, and she heard a new voice.

"Dear me. What to-do."

Drenched, the water globe washing against her knees and seeping into her shoes, Rhianna turned and looked.

A little man stood there, framed by the door and the light from outside. He wore a tall pointed hat, black but blazing with the signs of the moon and the sun and the stars. To balance the hat, he had a long pointed beard, like corn silk near his mouth, but white as snow elsewhere. It was long enough to tuck into his belt. The belt was jeweled, and there were more jewels sewn into his dark robe and cape. He held a staff of silver-gray wood in one hand.

"Water elemental, eh?" He smiled. "My, this must be an *advanced* class. In my day we didn't summon elementals until we passed third degree at Wizardly College."

Mrs. Greenapple dashed water out of her eyes. "We didn't summon . . . I mean, we didn't *mean* to . . ." Her voice was high and panicky.

"Didn't mean to?" The little man's eyebrows climbed. "Then this is an accident? Dear me, your spell wards must have failed completely. You really should be more careful, you know. Dangerous beasties, elementals."

The water globe heaved and rippled. It was as high as Rhianna's thigh now, and still growing.

The little man gazed at Rhianna, at the thundercloud, at the driving rain inside the classroom, and then at Mrs. Greenapple. It seemed as though he were looking at something interesting and cheerful, like a ride at a carnival. He took a closer grip on his staff. "I say," he asked, "would you like me to . . . ?" He glanced at the globe of water and made shooing-away gestures with the staff.

Mrs. Greenapple nodded rapidly. "Please, oh, please, Magister. I can't seem to . . ."

"Oh, of course not. No. Not with a stronger witch summoning it. Now let me think. Hmm. Yes, I see. Young

Lady" — to Rhianna — "just you think of . . . ah . . . dry toast, for a moment. *Dry* toast, mind. And no tea."

Rhianna thought of toast. Dry, hard toast, without butter.

The globe of water drew off a little way. The rain might have eased a little.

"Ah," said the wizard, approving. *Magister,* Mrs. Greenapple had called him. That meant *"master."* "That's right. Now." He flung his cape wide and his staff leaped into the air, drawing a fiery circle there. His voice came, powerful, driving, different from the vague and absent-minded way he had spoken before. *"Dehydra diminisha dranus desicca . . ."*

The globe of water stopped growing. It began to shrink. Rhianna thought of dry toast as hard as she could. The cloud also shrank and lost its intense blackness. After a moment it became gray, and then it began to break up into smaller wisps and tendrils, which faded away as she watched.

The globe became smaller and smaller, draining away into what was apparently thin air. The Magister continued to chant. The globe continued to shrink. At last there was a faint *pop!* and the water elemental, which had become a bead on the floor, disappeared.

The Magister stopped his chant. The three of them stood and stared at each other, Rhianna in dumb horror,

Mrs. Greenapple as though unable to believe her own eyes, and the little magician with a certain self-satisfaction.

"Well, that's that," he said. "Although I must say it wasn't easy. No wonder you're having trouble with magic drain hereabouts."

Mrs. Greenapple looked around her, openmouthed. Everything in the classroom was wet. Her good cape was dripping about her shoulders. Her hair hung in rats' tails. And the important visitor to the school, the one she had wanted so badly to impress, was watching her. Her eyes drifted over the utter ruin of her classroom — the soaked books, the stuffed pelican that would never be the same again, the chalk marks on the floor that had run into a milky puddle, the spellboard that had been given another, quite unneeded, washing.

Her gaze came to Rhianna, standing alone and dripping in the middle of the room. Her mouth closed. She didn't know *how,* she didn't understand *why,* but she did know *who.*

"Rhianna!" Mrs. Greenapple's voice didn't often crack like that. "Mrs. Wesbarrow's room. March!"

Rhianna's shoulders slumped. She had no idea what she'd done, but she could only agree with Mrs. Greenapple. It was clearly the most dreadful thing that had ever happened in the history of the school, and it was all her doing. Tears prickled at the corners of her eyes.

The little magician saw them. "No, no. Dear girl. Cheerful. Smile, please. No tears. You'll bring it back again, and we mustn't have that. Like calls to like, you know. Be angry, if you must be anything. At least anger is a fire caller. We really can't do with any more water just now. Laugh, please, if you can."

*Laugh?* Rhianna had never felt less like laughing. She had turned in obedience to Mrs. Greenapple's order, and was halfway to the door where the master magician was standing. For all his obvious power, his face had uncertainty in it.

She stopped. "Excuse me, please," she said. "I need to go to Mrs. Wesbarrow's room." The thought made her chin wobble again.

The little magician flapped his hands like someone trying to chase hens out of the house. "Oh, yes, I suppose so. We'd better go together. And" — he glanced at Mrs. Greenapple — "we'd best ask the young lady's parents to come to the school as well, don't you think?" He smiled as he said it. *Almost twinkled,* Rhianna thought.

Mrs. Greenapple's mouth thinned out and became a flat line. "Certainly, Magister. I was about to suggest that. I'll call them on the spellcaster myself."

The Magister beamed at her. "Excellent!" he said. "Now, miss, if you'll just come along with me. . . ."

They marched across the open green together,

Rhianna on the Magister's right, close by his staff. Children stood in groups, talking excitedly. Rhianna couldn't watch them.

They passed Rory Spellwright, who sniggered and said something under his breath to Merry Gladbetook. Both boys laughed, and Rory called out: "Rhianna's goin' to get expelled, hah!"

The Magister stopped and faced him. "Ah?" he asked, mildly. "You seem to know all about it, my young friend. Why would that happen?"

Merry had enough brains not to say anything, but Rory's mouth had always ruled his head. "'Cause she's so-o-o stupid. Really, really thick. She'll have to go back to the city, an' good riddance." He laughed again.

Rhianna felt her insides curl up. She wanted to go somewhere, anywhere, and die.

"You think so?" asked the Magister. "But then, you would think that. It's wrong, of course, but *foolishness comes from the mouths of fools.*" He seemed to grow suddenly taller, looming over them, dark and awesome. A cold wind sprang up out of nowhere. His voice deepened and took on the sound of distant thunder. "Your words are worth so little that I think it might be better if you spoke no more today, boy."

The staff in his hand started to glow. He raised it,

spoke a single word, and walked on. Rhianna went with him, looking over her shoulder at Rory and Merry.

Rory opened his mouth to speak, but nothing came out. Merry watched him with wide eyes. Still Rory tried to say something. He was *still* trying when Rhianna turned away from him.

"I do apologize for that," said the Magister. They had come to the door of Mrs. Wesbarrow's room. No one else was near, and Rhianna realized with a shock that the little magician was talking to her. He continued: "I really should keep my temper better." He tried to look severe with himself. "One must never use the power in anger, that's the first rule. You probably know that already."

Rhianna looked blank. She had never thought about such a thing.

"It was fun, though, you must admit," he went on, as though confessing to something. "And it will do that particular young fellow no harm at all to keep silence until the sun sets. By the way, my name is Northstar, Antheus Northstar. What's yours?"

Rhianna's mouth moved, just as Rory's had done. But she managed to find her voice. "Rhianna Wildwood, um, so please you, Magister."

He nodded vaguely. "Wildwood . . . Wildwood. That's your mother's name, of course. What was your father's?"

"Um . . . Periman, Magister."

"Ah. I should have known. Descendent of old Michaela Periman, I should think. High Witch of the White, and a great spellmaker. And Wildwood. Branch of the Hightree Wildwoods, I'll be bound. Strong High Elven strain on both sides, then. Your power's not to be wondered at."

*My power?* thought Rhianna bitterly. *My lack of power, you mean.* The knot in her stomach, which had slacked off a little, seemed to tighten again.

The Magister knocked twice on Mrs. Wesbarrow's door, and then threw it open and strode in. "Congratulations, colleague!" he boomed. "You must be very proud."

Mrs. Wesbarrow was a small, mousy woman with permanently pursed lips. She swung around from the spellcaster and blinked. "Proud?" she asked. *"Proud?"* Her eyebrows went up. "I've just been reading Ivy Greenapple's spellcast to Rhianna's parents. I can't imagine why you'd think I should be proud. Classroom soaked? *Water elemental?* Whatever next!" She glared at Rhianna. "You just wait until your parents get here, young lady. Why, I've a good mind to —"

Nobody would ever know what Mrs. Wesbarrow had a good mind to do. Magister Northstar's own eyebrows went up like snowflakes in a draft. "Dear lady," he said in the Wizard's Voice, the voice that stilled others, "I wonder if you understand what you have here. A Wild Talent is not seen frequently, but I had thought that teachers were trained to see the noses in front of their faces."

There was a moment of silence. "A Wild Talent?" Mrs. Wesbarrow asked, her voice high, almost squeaking. "I went to the lecture, but . . . a Wild Talent? I don't think I've ever seen one. Are you sure, Magister?"

Even Rhianna knew that one thing you must not do is ask a wizard what he knows or how he knows it. Magister Northstar frowned. "I am sure, madam," he said coldly, and that was the end of it.

# CHAPTER 4

Loys and Meg Wildwood arrived to find the school deserted, the children taken on a sudden outing, and Rhianna's classroom being mopped out by the school caretaker, old Mr. Moss. He directed them to Mrs. Wesbarrow's room. "She'll be there, for sure," he remarked, chuckling.

Meg looked at her husband, stricken.

Loys set his jaw. "I don't believe it. She wouldn't have done this — in fact, I don't think she *could* do it. But she wouldn't, and that's the important thing. They've got it wrong, you'll see. I'll sort it out."

Meg caught his arm. "Be polite to them, Loys," she said. "They can —"

"I know, I know." He knocked on the head teacher's door.

They were expecting to see Rhianna in the corner,

Mrs. Wesbarrow with a face of thunder, and a distinguished wizard looking outraged. But when the door opened, there was their daughter, sitting and eating elf-bread, and Mrs. Wesbarrow chuckling as if at a joke. As for the distinguished wizard, he was drinking tea and telling a story:

". . . never got over it, you know. Frogs everywhere. Frogs in the drainpipes, frogs in the sink. Frogs all over the spellroom floor. What was worse, they just kept popping out of nowhere. Hundreds of them. I have never seen a plague spell, you know, but I have an idea that it would be something like that. And that was the last, and only, time I saw a Wild Talent before today. At Wizardly College, when I was just a lad myself. Do you know, it took half the faculty to dispel the summoning, because the Talent couldn't stop thinking about frogs! Runes, books of spells, half a day of incantation, a pentacle of suppression, the lot. Never saw so much fuss. And the Talent, as I said, was a young fellow not quite right in the head . . ."

The Magister was seated in the only armchair, with his back to the door. Mrs. Wesbarrow glanced past him as the door opened. He noticed it, set his teacup down, and stood politely to meet the newcomers.

Rhianna stood, too, putting down her half-eaten

piece of elfbread. She had been enjoying herself, but the sight of her parents brought her troubles back with a rush.

"Rhianna?" her mother asked. "What *have* you been up to?"

The magician smiled. "Nothing at all, dear lady, except that she listened too carefully and copied her teacher too exactly."

There was a moment of silence, and then Mrs. Wesbarrow made introductions. Two more chairs had to be brought in. The little room was crowded. Magister Northstar resumed his place in the armchair. Although it was Mrs. Wesbarrow's room, there was no doubt who was in charge.

The Magister steepled his fingers and spoke. "Now, Mrs. and Mr. Wildwood. No doubt we shall have to confirm it, but there is no doubt in my mind, from the events of this morning, that your daughter is a Wild Talent. You've heard the term, I suppose?"

Loys and Meg glanced at each other. Both nodded.

Magister Northstar nodded in return. "But," he went on, "most people have never seen such a thing. A Wild Talent. Wild, meaning that it's difficult to control; Talent, meaning great power. I have a fair amount of power myself, but it has to be carefully shaped, like most people's. The right spells, the words and the pentacles and the conjurations and so forth. By using them, power can be called and then controlled. But Rhianna's Talent is more like the Old Magic, the magic that existed before the Magic Guild began to organize and channel it. It accepts no rules. It makes of itself what it wishes. Giving it spells and words and the rest only unleashes it, and the results can be frightening. That's what a Wild Talent is."

Loys and Meg exchanged another astonished glance. Meg leaned forward. "But, Magister, Rhianna . . . well, she's always had trouble with spells, and this year was worse than before. We were going to get her special tutoring."

The Magister waved one hand, palm towards her, as if to stop her from going on. "No, no, no! That would be the worst thing you could do. A Wild Talent? Special tutoring? Dear me! I'm very glad they called me in. In another year . . . well, who knows?" He took a sip of tea, and they watched him, frowning, puzzled.

He patted his lips with a napkin and continued. "Wild Talent is rare. There have been only two in the last thousand years with all their wits in the right place. One was the Archmagistra Selina of Sary."

"And the other?" Rhianna found herself asking him.

He turned and looked at her. "A man from Caradhas. You've never heard his name." His voice was flat certain.

Rhianna's puzzlement must have registered on her

face. The Magister's lips tightened. "He was never able to learn control. Or perhaps he never wanted to learn it. At any rate, he went to the bad, a thousand years ago. It took the College, the Queen's army, the Ring of the Sea, and the life of the hero Tam Longstrider to sink his black castle beneath the waves. And he may be there yet, brooding under the sea, waiting for the day when the Land is swallowed up by the waters and the Wild Magic is loosed on the world again."

The bright room darkened a little. There was silence, and the Magister brooded.

"And you're saying that Rhianna is like them?" Loys Wildwood hardly seemed to believe his own words.

The Magister shook himself. "Well. That much, I don't know and cannot say." He looked at Mrs. Wesbarrow. "What I *am* saying is that I'm sure she has a Wild Talent. It would explain much. As for having all her wits, I think you're the best judges of that."

There was another silence. Rhianna was thinking: *So maybe I'm not so dumb after all?*

"At any rate, it will be necessary to remove her from school for a few days while I do what I can. And then she must be taught in a special class. One of her own." Those calm words made everyone stare. Magister Northstar stared back, as if he had said nothing unusual. "Obviously," he added, and sipped his tea again.

"Ah . . ." Loys Wildwood looked doubtfully at his wife. "We did want her to have an education, Magister. Perhaps a special class would not be . . ."

"We have no such facilities . . ." began Mrs. Wesbarrow.

The wizard held up a hand. "Please. It will be a special class because she must learn different things from other children. Other children, with small power, as most of us have, must learn how to make the most of it. With Rhianna, the problem is different. She doesn't need spells and ingredients and pentacles and spellchanting. *She* must learn control — never to use any more magic than she absolutely must, never to take more than the least amount possible, and to bind with bands of iron what she does use." He smiled at Rhianna. "But she can learn the first steps here, among her friends. In years to come, perhaps, she will come to Wizardly College to study further."

Rhianna watched him, a little nervous of him despite the smile. "It sounds hard," she said.

He nodded. "It is. It is a difficult art, a hard road. But do you know, there is a law of magic: *Magic is never more than will.* If you will it so, you can control it. Your will is strong enough."

Meg leaned forward. "But what about a properly qualified teacher? No offense, Mrs. Wesbarrow."

The Magister pursed his lips. "Well, in one sense, I imagine that I am properly qualified to teach. At least, I should think so. If not, perhaps as Chancellor of Wizardly College, I could award myself some more diplomas. And so are her teachers here. In a different sense, though, nobody is qualified to teach Rhianna. A lot of what she must learn, she must come to herself." He frowned. "It is a lonely path, but she need not walk it entirely alone. I will go the first steps with her myself. Indeed, I think it would be best if I were to take her as an apprentice. It would give her a sort of bond with me, and another outlet for her power."

Silence. Loys cleared his throat. "Well, Magister, we'll think about what you say . . ."

The Magister was shaking his head. "I'm afraid there is no choice. Her power must be controlled, and it must be done now." He said it quietly, with sorrow.

Loys swelled, turning red. "What do you mean, no choice?" he demanded. "Look here, I don't know who you are, and I don't know who you *think* you are, but you can't just come in here . . ."

Magister Northstar gazed at him, his eyes huge and commanding, and the little room and the sunlight and the walls and the furniture faded away and were lost. Loys stuttered to a stop.

Magister Northstar spoke, his voice slow as ages and

heavy as doom. "I'm afraid I can, and I must." He sighed. "Although I do ask your pardon. I seem to have expressed myself poorly. When I said that there was no choice, I meant it not only for her." He turned to Rhianna, who sat gazing at him with her mouth open. "It's required, you see, for the Land itself."

Mrs. Wesbarrow took a hand. "Do you mean, Magister, that Rhianna's Talent must be tamed, or it will be a danger to her — and to others?"

"Mm? Oh, yes. That, too. But the real reason is quite different. You see, the country around here can't supply her."

"Can't supply her?"

"Yes. With enough power for her Talent. Talent seeks power, you see. Calls it up out of the ground, the air, the water. Rhianna's Talent is calling up that power and storing it. What might happen if it should all come out at once, I hate to think. But as she is taking up the power from the country around her, there's less for everyone else." He smiled a little. "They called me all this way to ask me why spells are failing hereabouts, and I walked in on the reason, not even knowing."

Loys and Meg stared at their daughter. Rhianna stared back. Her mind ran on like a rat in a cage.

Loys moistened his lips. "You mean . . . ?" he asked.

The Magister nodded. "Yes. The reason why your

spells are failing is sitting in that chair. It's Rhianna. And that's why I must do all in my power to control her magic. I will help her in any way I can, but by my oath as Wizard and as Mage on the Queen's Council, my first duty is to the Land and the Realm. That's what I meant about there being no choice. Control her power I must, or the Realm will suffer. And it must be done as soon as may be."

# CHAPTER 5

"Oh, dear Oh, *dear!* Oh, good heavens!"

Magister Northstar hopped from one foot to the other. A canary clung to the end of his staff. Two more settled on his pointed hat. Another dozen popped out of thin air in a whirl of lemon-yellow feathers. They joined the throng in front of Rhianna, whistling impatiently, pattering on the tiled floor. Small groups took off to fly around the room.

Rhianna stared at them in dismay. Already the kitchen of her house looked like the center of a lemon-drop snowstorm.

"Avaunt!" cried the Magister. "Rhianna, think of . . . um . . . something heavy. But don't think too hard." He made passes with his staff, the canaries fluttering around him. "Blast! The pentacle isn't holding them at all."

"The canaries aren't magical themselves, Magister," Rhianna reminded him.

"Oh, dear! Of course not. Get off! Shoo!" The canaries on his staff flew off to join the others, a whirling yellow cloud. More kept appearing, though not as fast. "Now. *Unflutter by butterfly unwingless belessing . . .*"

Rhianna thought of heavy things. Big, clumsy, gray, heavy things. Then, because she did not want to start summoning elephants, she thought of stars and planets, and then of other things as far removed from canaries as possible. The Magister chanted, and the flow of canaries slowed, became a trickle, and finally stopped. He chanted another line to make sure before falling silent, pushing back his tall hat and wiping his forehead on a large cotton handkerchief he had pulled from the pocket of his robe. Finally he used his staff to trace the rune Liss, the rune of guarding, on the place in the air where the canaries had been appearing. Glowing slightly, it hovered for a few moments before fading.

The Magister found a chair and collapsed onto it, fanning himself with his hat. Canaries flew in clouds around the room, piping and calling. The air was full of the sound of whirring wings.

"Open a window or two, there's a girl," he said. "That unsummoning spell has quite drained me. You're getting stronger all the time, you know."

Rhianna jumped up and did as he asked. The butter-colored cloud began to thin as canaries in singles, pairs, and small groups took their leave, flying out of the windows. Magister Northstar looked up at them fluttering into the bright sky. "Thank heavens it isn't nighttime," he said after a minute or so. "We'd never get rid of them." He pulled his hat on again. "Right, now. How did that happen? We were supposed to be getting lemons, you know. Not much harm in lemons, and you can sell them." He looked at Rhianna severely.

Rhianna started to hunch her shoulders, just as she used to, but she remembered that Magister Northstar disliked that habit very much. She tried not to scowl, as well. Still, it was difficult to stare straight at him. "I — I think it was the birds singing in the trees outside while I said the spell, Magister. I thought, just for a moment, how pretty they sounded, and it got mixed-up with the lemons in my mind, and so . . ."

"We got a flock of lemon-colored birds. A great big flock of them." Magister Northstar nodded. "Well, it makes sense. I suppose I should be thankful that we're not close enough to the river for you to hear the sound of the water. We'd have drowned before I could have done anything sensible. And in lemonade, too. Well, you'd best come away. So strong a summoning must have lowered your own reserves, for the time being."

He pushed open the door and ushered Rhianna out into the back garden. Once there, he muttered a simple call spell, and the remaining canaries flew out of the windows in clouds. They settled on the grass in front of him or perched in nearby hedges, whistling and calling. "Is that all of them?" he asked wearily.

Rhianna looked, and nodded.

The Magister let the spell lapse and the birds began to fly off in all directions. Then he stood, leaning on his staff for a moment. "Come along, Rhianna," he said.

They passed through the back gate and into the meadow beyond, the Magister silent, walking, his staff making his pace. Rhianna was silent, too. She twisted her fingers together and wondered what she could do to make things better.

"Control, Rhianna," the Magister said after a while. "How is it to be controlled?" He walked on a few more paces. "That was a case of using too much magic," he said. "You put too much power into the summoning spell. And the summon wasn't exact enough. You didn't have the right thing in your mind."

He frowned, then stopped short. "The right thing in your mind?" he murmured. "Or the thing right in your mind? Hmm. I wonder." He pulled off his hat, looked at it, and put it back on again. "I asked you to summon lemons. How often do you see lemons?"

Rhianna shrugged. "Not very often, Magister. There

are no lemon trees here — I think it's too cold for them. But I know what lemons look like. There's a picture in one of my books."

The Magister nodded. "Ah. I think I see. And I understand what my error was. How could I ask you to summon something you knew only from pictures? You have to . . . ah! That's it!" He clapped his hands together, a sharp sound, letting go of his staff to do it. The staff stayed in place, upright.

Rhianna watched him. He was squinting off into the distance, where the sun shone above the far hills.

They were on the top of the slope that led down to the village. Smallhaven lay in a little valley that ran down to the sea. Rhianna's home was up on the slope above the village, and from the meadow you could look down onto the cottage roofs. You could see the pier where fishing boats unloaded their catch, a row of houses along the harbor wall, and then the single cobbled street that led away from the shore like the downstroke on the letter T. The school, the inn, and the few shops — and Loys Wildwood's smithy — lined that street, before it broadened out to become the village green and marketplace. Around the green stood more houses, and then the street became a road that turned left and wandered up the valley toward the farms and the hills. Beyond the hills, tall mountains ranged, blue with distance, snowcapped. Wild country lay out there, with strange people and stranger things than they. Trolls, some said. Faerie folk. Dragons.

Magister Northstar stared as if he wasn't watching any of that. He was stroking his beard. Then he nodded once, sharply. "We'll try again tomorrow, Rhianna, when I have finished the binding spell to apprentice you. I need some ivy tendrils and a swan's feather for that. I suppose the spell shop in the village will have them. Come to think of it, I'll need Mr. Spellwright's signature on the apprenticeship paper. It has to be witnessed by a wizard. When I've done that, I'll have some control over your magic, and I'll set you a task that should be a little easier."

Rhianna said nothing. She wasn't sure she understood, exactly.

The next morning, the Magister came early to the Wildwoods' cottage, and he and Rhianna walked down to the village with Meg, who would sign the papers, too. They waved to Loys, who was hard at work in the smithy, and then crossed the street and entered the spell shop.

It was as if Mr. Spellwright hadn't moved since Rhianna had seen him last. He was leaning on his counter, gazing towards the door. The shop, as usual, was dim and cool, although the morning sun was bright at the windows.

Magister Northstar nodded politely, and an odd sort of expression came to Mr. Spellwright's face. A frown, almost, but then it cleared, and his mouth stretched sideways. A gold tooth winked in the gloom. Rhianna realized that Mr. Spellwright was smiling. He removed his hands from the counter and clasped them in front of his chest, bending slightly from the waist.

"Good morning, colleague!" Magister Northstar greeted him. "I wonder if you could oblige me with two handspans of ivy tendrils — fresh, if you have them, but dried will do — and a swan's pinion feather. A mute swan, mind. For a binding spell for an apprentice, you understand."

Mr. Spellwright stopped smiling. He looked from Magister Northstar to Rhianna and then back again. He blinked, and it couldn't have been because of the light. "An apprentice binding? For her?" he asked.

"Yes, indeed. For Rhianna. I'll be apprenticing her — and I'm certain that the village will have cause to be proud of her. And I'll ask you to witness the paper, if you would."

Mr. Spellwright moistened his lips, made to speak, hesitated, and then leaned forward, as if to speak privately into Magister Northstar's ear. But the Magister drew back, and Mr. Spellwright had no choice but to say it out loud: "Well, actually, Magister, I was meaning to ask you about apprenticing my nephew Rory. A smart lad, that, well ahead in his studies. I'm sure he'd make a fine —"

The Magister shook his head. "I'm sorry, colleague, but I do not normally accept apprentices. Miss Wildwood here is a special case. No doubt your nephew is a fine student; I'll send you the names of any of the magicians in Avalon who are looking for an apprentice. But for now, all I need is the ingredients I mentioned, if you would oblige me, please."

Mr. Spellwright straightened. He tugged at his apron. His eyes rested for a moment on Rhianna and her mother, and then returned to Magister Northstar. The Magister raised one tufted eyebrow, just a little, and Mr. Spellwright nodded jerkily.

"Just a moment," he mumbled. "Not much call for swan feathers. They're at the back."

He had to use a pair of steps to bring a jar down from a top shelf, but he produced a long white feather and a moment later some pieces of dried tendril that Rhianna supposed must be ivy. She knew what these were for: ivy to bind, a mute swan's feather to keep secrets.

Magister Northstar nodded his thanks and put down a silver coin. He drew a rolled-up paper from his pocket and placed it flat on the counter, where Mr. Spellwright had a quill pen and ink. The Magister dipped the quill in the ink and signed his name at the bottom of the paper.

"You sign here, Rhianna . . . that's right. Now you, Mrs. Wildwood. Thank you. And now, if you would witness it, Mr. Spellwright . . . ?"

Mr. Spellwright took the quill and looked down at the paper. He coughed. "Are you quite sure about this, Magister . . . colleague? It seems a little —"

Magister Northstar raised both eyebrows this time. He studied Mr. Spellwright's face as if he wanted to remember it. "I thank you for your opinion, Mr. Spellwright, even though I did not ask for it. But I am quite sure. I only require you to witness the deed, not to approve of it. Please do as I ask."

Rhianna heard the chill in his voice. She hoped she would never hear it meant for her.

Mr. Spellwright hesitated a bare moment longer, then bent and signed the paper in a hurried scrawl.

Magister Northstar blew on the ink to dry it, and then carefully tore it down the center. He gave one half to Rhianna, and put the other in his pocket. He nodded to Mr. Spellwright. "I thank you," he said coolly. "Come, Rhianna. There's a good charcoal fire in your father's forge. Good day, Mr. Spellwright."

# CHAPTER 6

Unlike Mr. Spellwright's shop, the smithy was always warm. It was sunlit, too, with an open front so that you could watch people passing in the street. Folk walked by, and most waved or called a greeting. A long, narrow charcoal fire burned in a brick tub, and Loys Wildwood pumped the bellows with his foot to heat iron until it glowed like the setting sun before he beat it into shape with his hammers.

He was finishing a set of firedogs when his wife and daughter came in with the Magister, and they watched as he shaped the bar iron. Firedogs were racks to hold a burning log in a fireplace. They were just iron bars, really, but they stood on either side of the fire, and they were made to look like long, thin dogs, with noses and tails that pointed upward to hold the log in place. Rhianna smiled as she saw them emerge, paws and eyes and ears and noses, under her father's skilled hands. Or rather, under his hammer, nippers, chisel, and punch, for these dogs were made of red-hot iron. Blacksmithing was a great skill, and it suddenly came to her that it was as great and as useful as magic itself.

Loys held the glowing iron in his tongs, looked at it from various angles, and nodded, satisfied. He plunged the finished dog into the water barrel to quench it, and a cloud of steam went up.

"I've always wondered how they did that," said Magister Northstar, admiration in his voice.

Loys Wildwood laughed. "No great trick for a wizard, sir," he said. He wiped his brow with a handful of tow, his broad face good-humored.

"I wouldn't say that," answered the Magister. "I couldn't make so much as an iron nail, and I have the feeling that cold iron may be more than my art, in time to come. But we have come to do some magic here. I didn't feel like doing it in Spellwright's shop."

"Just imagine, Loys," said Meg, "Mr. Spellwright wanted Magister Northstar to apprentice Rory, his nephew, instead of Rhianna. He was quite insistent."

"Rory Spellwright? The one with the shifty eyes?" Loys looked annoyed. "You, er, didn't . . ."

"No, I did not," answered Magister Northstar stoutly.

"And I am about to work the apprentice binding here and now. I wonder if I might borrow the fire, just for a moment. So long as I touch no iron, it should be perfect."

The apprenticing spell took only a few minutes. Magister Northstar said the words, the ivy and the feather were burned, and master and new apprentice breathed in a little of the smoke. Rhianna's parents watched with pride as their daughter was made into the official pupil of the highest wizard in the Realm. They knew, and she knew, that her life would never be the same again.

Still, Magister Northstar's eyes widened as some of Rhianna's power flowed into him, and his staff flared a little. "Whoo!" he puffed. Color came and went in his cheeks. "Just as well I was fairly drained. You're like a roaring great fire, Rhianna. We'll have to try to cool you off before you cook yourself."

Rhianna nodded. She didn't want to be cooked. And she was eager to get on. They took leave of the smithy, Loys Wildwood tousling his daughter's hair with a big, gentle hand.

They returned to the cottage and sat at the kitchen table. They would not be summoning lemons this time, Magister Northstar explained.

"Control, Rhianna. You need to control. There's only one way to control, and that's to shape the magic you use just exactly right for whatever you want to use it for.

Never too much of it, never the wrong shape or size or style or type. To know those things, to know just how much to use, you must know exactly the thing you are trying to spell. Other people can afford to be sloppy. For them, it hardly matters. Not you. Your knowledge must be exact."

"Exact?" Rhianna's ears pricked up. "I can be exact? I can say exactly what I mean?"

He nodded. "Yes. That's what you have to do. Any magic that doesn't exactly fit the spell is uncontrolled. And it would be very bad if your magic went out of control."

He frowned, but Rhianna almost laughed. *How funny,* she thought. *All I ever wanted was to have rules that made sense and didn't change. And now I've got one.*

"So," he continued, "we need to start you off with something you know very well indeed. Something you see every day, something that's part of you. But nothing too heavy or sharp or dangerous. What's that yeasty smell, Mrs. Wildwood, by the way?"

Meg smiled. "It's the bread sitting in the pan by the window, Magister. I've just punched it down so it's ready for its second rising. Now, I'll leave you to it. I have to pick some beans for dinner." She stepped outside.

Magister Northstar removed the cloth that covered the bread dough and brought the pan over to the table.

"The very thing. What could be simpler, what could be more familiar, or safer, than rising bread? Eh, Rhianna?"

Rhianna nodded doubtfully. It was true, she had helped her mother knead dough and bake bread before. It was something she was familiar with, and a rising spell wasn't difficult. A good cook could produce a sponge cake so light it nearly floated away.

They went over what she needed to do. No words or spells. She would use the Wild Magic on its own, just a very little of it, to make the bread rise. Magister North-star readied a counterspell and nodded.

Rhianna concentrated on the bread dough. It stirred slightly. She reached out for it in her mind and felt how it was, warm and squishy and heavy. It should be lighter, more airy.

As she thought that, she felt a trickle of magic. Just the tiniest bit. The dough began to rise slowly, getting larger and bulkier. Rhianna grinned. It was working!

The dough shook itself, trembled, seemed to quiver — and then it slowly unstuck itself from the bread pan and began to float gently up toward the ceiling. Rhianna shook her head at it. That wasn't supposed to happen! *Not like that. I said light, but not so light you float.* The dough darkened alarmingly, becoming shiny and solid. Rhianna frowned. *No, no, you're supposed to rise. Not like that.* She made a movement and her concentration broke. The magic tumbled out of her like water over the top of a dam.

The dough shot up, obeying Rhianna's last thought. It took off like a rocket, faster and faster, streaking towards the ceiling. Rhianna jerked her head up to follow it, but it was only a brown blur when it hit. There was a loud crack, a rending crash, and, just after that, another crashing sound. Plaster and bits of wood rained down. Then a slate, from the roof above their heads. It fell through the hole in the ceiling and shattered on the floor.

Magister Northstar jumped and peered upwards. Plaster dust was still sifting down, but he squinted through the hole in the roof into the patch of bright blue sky overhead. When nothing more happened, he slumped in relief.

He turned to see Meg Wildwood standing in the doorway, openmouthed, staring at the hole in her kitchen ceiling.

Magister Northstar winced. Again he looked after the rocketing ball of dough. "I can't see it anymore. I doubt if it'll stop before it reaches the moon," he remarked, and then, to Meg, "I do apologize, dear lady. My fault entirely. I'll just step down to the village and ask the local tiler to call around and repair the hole. I'm sure he will drop everything else for me. I'll call in at the baker's, too, for another loaf of bread. Come along, Rhianna."

And he hustled her out the door before her mother could say anything.

On the road, he removed his hat, scratched his head, and looked at Rhianna. "Well, that does it. I was watching every moment, and I didn't have a chance to do anything sensible at all. It happened too fast for either of us. You have too much power. It's like trying to paper over a volcano."

Rhianna couldn't hide her disappointment. Her lip trembled. A fat tear escaped and rolled down her cheek. "It was going so well, at first," she faltered. Magister Northstar offered her his handkerchief, and she wiped her eyes.

"There, there." He patted her shoulder. "It's not your fault. It's the magic itself. It won't be confined or controlled. It insists on coming out in larger and larger amounts, just as it wants to." But he was speaking in a distracted sort of way, and it was clear that he was worried.

"What can I do?" wailed Rhianna. "It's too strong for me. It feels as if I'm trying to ride a horse that I can't control — and it keeps running away with me." She wiped her eyes again.

The wizard stroked his beard. He nodded. "You're right. I was a fool to think you could manage this in a week or two. Nobody could do that. It's my own fault. I had no idea how hard it would be."

Rhianna sniffled into the handkerchief. Magister Northstar watched her sympathetically. They stopped walking and stood under a shady tree, so that nobody would see her.

"There's nothing else for it," the Magister continued, after a moment. "You're too strong. If this goes on . . . well, anything might happen. Like that water elemental you called. There are other things that might answer when you call, and many of them are worse than elementals. Much worse." He shuddered, and a shadow fell over the sunny sky. The mountains loomed blue in the distance. He seemed to shake himself. "If it will not allow control, then it must be shackled, just as you tie up a horse that kicks."

"Shackled?"

"Yes. I don't like it, because so great a Talent as yours, Rhianna, should be used. But so be it. We can delay no longer."

Rhianna felt her face grow tight around the eyes. He noticed it. "Oh, don't worry," he soothed her. "I won't take your gift away. Indeed, I can't. But we have to stop what it's doing — collecting power from everything around you. You're taking up much of the supply for the whole district, you know. The more power you collect, the more it's going to overflow — and there's no knowing where it will go, or what it will do."

"So," Rhianna asked carefully, "what will *you* do?"

He sighed and looked away. "It will mean a special sort of spell. Power comes from the Land, from the earth, the water, and the air. Well, what we will do is make a device, a thing you wear all the time, like a ring or a locket. It will be pretty — I'm sure I can choose something that you will like — but it will have a spell on it. We can't stop your Talent from taking up power, but we can store the power in the jewel, and then empty it out from time to time, like bailing water out of a boat. Better to fix the boat so that it doesn't leak, but at least bailing it out stops it from sinking. As long as you bail the water out as fast as it comes in."

Rhianna thought about it. "But if you did that, I'd have no magic at all."

Magister Northstar looked down and shuffled his feet. "Um. Yes. That's true. But if we do it any other way, the power will simply build up again. Until it overflows again. And sinks your boat."

"Oh." Rhianna frowned.

Magister Northstar misunderstood the frown. "Um . . . yes, I can see how that would worry you." He smiled, a little uncertainly.

Rhianna's head was aching, and a tight little dry feeling scratched at the back of her eyes. It had been a long week, and a hard one. "You're worried about what will happen if I don't wear this thing all the time," she said. "Worried that I'll be difficult about it. Because if I am, you won't know what to do next."

Magister Northstar raised his eyebrows. His staff was leaning against the tree, as always within his reach. His hand moved toward it, and then withdrew. For a moment he had seemed to grow taller, just as he had when he had struck Rory Spellwright dumb. Then he sighed, and the moment passed.

"I'll try no wizardly tricks on you, Rhianna," he said. "No fooling, either. You're too sharp, and anyway, you're my apprentice."

Watching him, Rhianna suddenly saw that he was indeed only a little man, and that his spangled robe and his staff and his tall hat didn't really matter. What mattered was that he was a wizard on the inside as well.

It was with his eyes on the staff that the Magister spoke: "I am the Chancellor of Wizardly College and the Mage on the Queen's Council. I speak for the magic of the Realm. You are my apprentice, and I am responsible for you. I will not allow you to come to harm; and yet my first duty is to the Realm itself." He looked at Rhianna. "And you are a danger to it."

Rhianna's lip quivered. "I don't —" she started.

He waved a hand. "Oh, you don't mean to be. Not at all. I know you now, Rhianna Wildwood, and I'd trust your heart to the end of the world. But magic needs more than heart. It needs a firm, sure hand. It needs skill. You will learn the skill — but until you do, you are in danger, and you are dangerous." He sighed. "So far, the things that have gone wrong have been little things, and funny, really. But sooner or later something serious will happen. It might be anything, but whatever it is, it will be wild and strong. Fearful, too. At least, *I* fear it."

Rhianna nodded. "I fear it, too, Magister," she said.

"That's wise. So will you wear this trinket?"

She thought, and then decided. "Yes," she said.

# CHAPTER 7

"It's the Law of Magical Means," said Magister Northstar. "The greater the magic, the more costly the piece. Rhianna's power is very great, though at present uncontrolled. The magic of any jewel that stores it will take the whole College the better part of a day to make, and therefore the piece must be of the very highest quality. I must go at once to have it made — in Avalon. I'll be sailing on the evening tide. There is no time to waste."

It was later that day. Magister Northstar was explaining matters to Rhianna's parents. He sipped rushwash tea and sat back. They looked at him, and then at each other.

"Will Rhianna be going with you?" asked Loys, in the sort of voice that meant he was going to argue if Magister Northstar said yes.

The little wizard shook his head. "I would not take a child from her family and home without the clearest need. I'll go myself, have the jewel made and bespelled, and send it back with some other things. Lessons for Rhianna, and a spellcaster that will reach me at any hour of the day or night."

He sighed. "I've been away longer than I planned. There'll be a mountain of work on my desk, and in three days there is the monthly meeting of the Queen's Council. I cannot miss that." He smiled at Rhianna. "I'll look in again as soon as I can — within a month, hopefully. Meanwhile, wear the jewel that I shall send. Do the lessons — you can work on them at school. I'll send them to your teacher. You must go to Mr. Spellwright every week to have the jewel drained of magic. He can do that. I've just spent some time instructing him. An odd fellow."

Later they saw Magister Northstar down to the harbor. It was evening, and the first stars were twinkling. The ship that would take him across the water to Home Island and Avalon was waiting.

At the head of the pier Magister Northstar put a hand briefly on Rhianna's brow. "A blessing," he murmured. "And no taking the jewel off, Rhianna. Not until you've mastered your magic. Mr. Spellwright will have a lot to drain and return, I can see that. Good night to you all. Expect my packet in four days."

He turned and stepped down into the ship. The sailors cast off, and the sail rose to the evening breeze.

The steersman leaned on the tiller. A few moments later Rhianna could see nothing of the wizard but the pale glow of his staff. It lifted in farewell.

Rhianna spent the four days fretting and waiting, thinking about magic as little as possible. But on the fourth day the packet arrived, as well as another one addressed to Mrs. Wesbarrow at the school.

There were two small boxes and a letter in the Wildwoods' parcel. The letter read:

*Greetings.*

*Please forgive this short scribble. Here is the magic-storing jewel I promised. Rhianna is to wear it at all times except when it is being drained out. Here, also, is the spellcaster, which has its own instructions. If there is any problem, any problem at all, you are to call me at once, at any hour.*

*I have sent lessons to Rhianna's teacher. We will be starting with simple, familiar things — the meadows around your own house. I will check with her, and with you, every week, by spellcast.*

*Remember, Rhianna, exactness. If you are to achieve control, you must know exactly what you are trying to do.*

*In haste,*
*A. Northstar.*

One of the boxes was small, square, and wooden. In it was a globe of glass and a slip of paper. Meg read the paper and nodded.

"Not too difficult," she said. "What's in the other?"

It was a flat boxwood case with a clasp. Rhianna opened it, and it was as if the sun had just peeped above the sea. She heard her mother's sudden inward breath.

Lying on a silk lining was a pendant on a chain. The chain was fine gold. In every third link a deep red stone glowed like a drop of blood, and in the middle of the chain . . .

It was a rune, the rune Liss, the sign of warding and guarding, a shape like a straighter letter S turned on its side, with two dots, one inside each curve. But this shape was made of gold, and the two dots were jewels, larger than the others. They had fire like a dragon's heart at their centers.

It was the most beautiful work of hands that Rhianna had ever seen. She reached out a finger to it, almost fearing to touch it, and then looked up at her mother.

Meg Wildwood's face showed her amazement. "He asked what your birthday was. June the twenty-third, a fire month and a fire day. Your birthstone is the greatest of the fire stones: ruby. You were born on a Sunday, the day of gold. I'd say that jewel is made of real rubies and solid gold. It must be almost beyond price, something fit for the Queen to wear." She was whispering, as though she feared to make noise.

Rhianna looked down at the beautiful thing in the box. A little voice sounded in her mind: *Don't forget, this is to stop you from having any magic at all. This is to take it all away.* She reached out and picked it up. It lay warm in her hand.

The moment she touched it, it seemed to her that a background noise she had always heard had stopped. It was as if there were some change in the light of the day. She looked around at the familiar kitchen and it was just the same. The sun was not less bright, but something was different.

*Well, what else would you expect?* she asked herself. The jewel was magical, after all. She put the chain around her neck so that the rune sparkled at her throat.

"Do up the clasp for me, please, Mother," she said.

Two weeks later Rhianna lay on her stomach, her workbook open in front of her, in the grassy meadow by the schoolhouse. Her class was learning Spellcasting this morning, but she had her own work to do.

She was drawing a long grass leaf that she had plucked. She drew it with great care, the tip of her tongue showing between her teeth, trying to get the shape and the size and the parts of the leaf all exactly right. It took a long time.

There were so many things to learn. There were hundreds of different kinds of grass in every field, all of them with different leaves and heads and growth and seeds. It would soon be summer, and they were all in different stages of sprouting and setting. But she had to know them all, in all their parts. If she ever wished to use magic on grasses, she must know every leaf and every shoot of them. And grasses were just the beginning.

The drawing went slowly, but it felt sure, and it looked right. The more closely she looked at the leaf, the more she saw, and the more she understood.

Everything was like that, she thought. The clouds over her head and the pebbles under her feet. The trees that covered the hills and the hawk on the wind. All of it was rich and full of details that she had to find out and understand perfectly before she could begin to work magic. Yet that was all right, in its way. It was a thing she could understand, not like the nonsense words in the spells she had to learn at school.

Only the flies bothered her, and saying the little spell that kept them off made no difference now, not with the pendant taking away all her magic. Rhianna shook her head, partly to get rid of a fly, partly from annoyance. She wished she could just be like everyone else. It had been fun telling her class about the jewel and what it was for, and everyone had admired it, but still . . .

The drawing was finished. Rhianna wrote a name for every part, and then she compared the drawing with the real leaf. They looked exactly alike. She glanced around. Perhaps she could give herself a test on it.

She closed her book and held the leaf up, checking every part, every shade of color, every vein and bend. She was sure she had it right.

She looked around once more, and then she slipped the pendant chain over her head and laid it on the grass beside her. She felt the magic filling her up, like a rising tide from all around, from the earth and the air and the trees. It was — normal. She *should* feel like this. The jewel was beautiful, but when it was around her neck, it was as if she were deaf and blind. Now she could feel the magic. She had never done that before. *Just like fish,* she thought. *I'll bet they don't feel the water.*

She looked at the leaf again, and when she was absolutely sure, she shaped a little of the magic around her. Just a little. No spell was needed, no passes with the hands. The magic was in her and worked through her, and she thought of exactly how the leaf was, and then of exactly how she wanted it to be.

The leaf trembled, and then it curled gently into a

circle. At the same time a different color washed up from the stalk. Spring-fresh green became gold. The gold brightened until it was the metal of the pendant, rich and sparkling, with the tiny veins a darker, goldlike toffee. The tip of the leaf touched the stalk. It had become what Rhianna wanted it to be — a thin golden bangle in the form of a leaf curled into a circle. The droplets of dew had turned into tiny shimmering crystals. A beautiful jewel, and she had made it.

A feeling of wonder rushed over her, like diving into a pool. *She* had done this thing. She had changed the leaf. By changing it, she had changed the world.

She held in her mind just how the leaf had been, checking against the drawing in the book. Then she used just a tiny bit more of the magic that flowed in from all sides. The golden bangle relaxed and straightened and flushed a spring-green and was a leaf again. And no more.

Rhianna laughed, and slid the pendant over her head again. In an instant the magic disappeared, like a light blown out. But now she knew. She knew what she could do, and she knew how to do it. Magister Northstar was right. It was hard, and it took great exactness, but it could be done.

Now, what about burdock? How were its leaves different? She started another drawing.

When the bell rang for lunch, she put her book away and sat with Rose in their usual place.

"I think you ought to know," said Rose, opening her lunch basket, "that Rory Spellwright got into trouble this morning."

"You're breaking my heart," said Rhianna with a grin.

But Rose was frowning. "No, really. Mrs. Greenapple told him off for daydreaming. He was staring out of the window."

"Rory? He never daydreams. He's not the daydreaming type."

"You're right. He's always too busy looking out for himself. But I had a look out of the window, too, and I saw you drawing in your book."

Rhianna paused, an apple halfway to her mouth. "He was looking out of the window at *me*?"

"Yes. Odd, isn't it?"

*Did Rory see me take the pendant off?* Rhianna wondered. And then she thought: *No, he couldn't have, because if he had, he'd have told Mrs. Greenapple as fast as he could put his hand up.*

Just as she thought that, a shadow fell across her. She looked up. There, looming over her, was Rory himself.

"Rhianna. We need to talk," he said. He smiled brightly.

Rhianna shrugged. She didn't trust that smile. "So talk."

"In private." He flicked a glance at Rose.

Rose glared at him. "Say it, Rory, and go away," she told him. "Or, better still, just go away."

Rory shook his head. "Rhianna wouldn't want me to say this in public, would you, Rhianna? You wouldn't want me to tell people what I saw, eh?"

Rhianna's heart sank. Rory had always had that effect on her. But when she looked at his face, she knew suddenly that she couldn't let him do it anymore. Rose was gazing at her, and her eyes were questioning.

Rhianna swallowed. "Rose, what Rory means is that he saw me take the pendant off, just for a minute. I shouldn't have done it."

Rory blinked. He hadn't expected that. But he came back quickly. "You didn't just take it off. You made something right there. Something real nice." He smirked as Rhianna went rigid. "Relax. I don't have to tell anyone you did it. See? I can be nice to you. And what I reckon is, if I'm nice to you, you should be nice back to me. Thing is, it seems you can make all sorts of stuff. Now me, I could really use a new penknife, and maybe one of those little crossbows, and a few —"

"Forget it, Rory." Rhianna's voice surprised even her. It was hard and unbending; perhaps it had a bit of the

Magister's own power in it. "I made a mistake. I'm not making another. Go peddle your goods somewhere else."

Rory's face went still, but his eyes flickered. "What are you going to say to Mrs. Greenapple, then, when I tell her?"

Rhianna sighed. "I'll tell her the truth, Rory. The jewel stores all my magic and your uncle empties it out every week. I took it off once, and never again. The end. Now go away. You annoy me."

"Yes," said Rose. "Go ahead and tell, Rory. It'll get you nothing."

"You watch. I will, I'll tell . . ." Rory started to back off, his eyes hard as stones. And then he stopped. He was still for a moment, and his face cleared. He nodded, smiled, turned, and walked away.

"I'll back you up," said Rose. "I'll tell Mrs. Greenapple you never took it off at all. He's just a liar. Everyone knows it."

Rhianna's voice was stubborn. "No. It won't do. If I'm asked, I'll tell the truth."

The day passed. Mrs. Greenapple said nothing to Rhianna other than "Good work" when she saw the workbook. Nothing happened at all, and there was Rory at his desk, still smiling. Rhianna wished she knew what he was smiling about.

*    *    *

At the end of the week, Rhianna had three pages of drawings in her workbook, and Mrs. Greenapple had given her a gold star for them. Magister Northstar would be pleased with her. And then it was time to take the jewel to Mr. Spellwright to have the magic emptied from it and returned to the ground.

Rhianna's mother walked with her down to the spell shop. "I'll just pop down to the market while you have your pendant emptied out," she said. "Mr. Spellwright said it wouldn't take long. Meet me at the market when you've finished." She nodded at another shopper who was passing. "Good morning, Mrs. Brewer."

Mrs. Brewer sniffed, and walked on briskly without a word. Meg looked after her, openmouthed.

"Yes, Mother," said Rhianna. She pushed open the door with its bell that tinkled, and went into the shop.

Inside it was cool and dark as always. Rhianna looked around her. Minor charms in bundles, herbs, magic spell ingredients. Witchlights, alarums, refilling bottles, healing bandages, horse quieteners, ripening salve, wart removers, tonics, chillers, firetouch sticks. And those odd jars with still stranger things in them. And Mr. Spellwright, leaning on his counter.

"Good morning, Mr. Spellwright," said Rhianna. Mr. Spellwright didn't move, but Rhianna saw his eyes swivel towards her. "I've come to have my magic emptied," she continued.

Mr. Spellwright's hand slid across the counter, pale in the gloom, and opened, palm up. He said nothing.

Rhianna took off the pendant and laid it in the open palm. The chain flowed over it, a spill of bright gold, the rubies glowing. Mr. Spellwright's fingers closed. He pulled himself upright, running the gold between his fingers.

"Wait here," he said. "And don't touch anything."

He shuffled into the back of the shop, passed through an open door there, and pulled it shut behind him. Rhianna could hear a scraping noise, and then a light showed under the door. As she watched, the light slowly changed color, from the normal bright yellow of a candle flame to a sharp mint-green.

She sighed, found a stool by the counter, and sat down on it.

Minutes passed. The green light slowly dimmed, then flared suddenly, once, twice. There was a tinkle, a jingling. The light grew softer, lighter. It went back to being a warm yellow. Then, suddenly, it went out altogether.

After a short pause, footsteps sounded. The door opened. Mr. Spellwright stepped out, and Rhianna saw a smile on his face. When he saw her, the smile went out as sharply as a snuffed candle.

Without words, he held out the pendant, the jewels dangling from his hand like sparks. She took it and put it on.

"Same time, same day next week. Without fail," said Mr. Spellwright. He was looking straight over Rhianna's head.

She nodded. "Yes. Thank you, Mr. Spellwright," she said. He didn't respond, but just stood watching her. She pulled open the front door and, turning, saw him hurry into the back of the shop again as she went out into the street.

Meg Wildwood was buying apples in the market. Cooking apples, for a pie. Rhianna smiled at that as she walked up to her.

As she came into earshot, she realized that her mother was unhappy. "You're asking twice as much for apples as you did last week," she said to the stallholder.

"Prices go up, Mrs. Wildwood," said the stallholder. He looked at Rhianna and his face was cold. "There's been a lot of brown spot on the fruit. Ripening spell failed, I hear."

Meg shook her head. "I'll take only three," she said. "It'll be a small pie."

The stallholder shrugged, and thrust three apples into a bag. He held out a hand for the money before he handed them over.

Meg took the bag and walked away, looking puzzled. "What's got into people?" she asked.

Rhianna didn't answer. She didn't know either. But she saw that her mother was hurt and bewildered. She took her hand and gave it a squeeze. Meg smiled, and they climbed the hill towards home.

# CHAPTER 8

Weeks passed. Rhianna's workbook filled up, and she started a new one. She drew and learned about all the plants of the meadows: the grasses, the small flowers, the clovers, the weeds. She knew them by leaf and stem, bud and flower and seed, their colors, their patterns, the way they grew. Next month, maybe, she would start on shrubs and bushes. Then, as autumn came on, she would learn about the leaves of the trees as they changed. In winter, about water — rain and snow and ice, rivers and streams. And more, and more. Her head spun at the thought of all there was to know.

Each week, on Tuesday, she went to Mr. Spell-wright's shop, and it was always the same. He sniffed, took her pendant into his back room, did whatever he did, came back, and returned it to her without a word, looking straight past her the whole time. Rhianna had never liked going into that odd shop with its dried-herb smell and its strange things in jars. Now she liked it less than ever.

Then the storm broke, and she had no idea that it had been building up.

One afternoon her father came home early. He was calm, too calm, and the expression on his face was flat and controlled, not open and friendly as it usually was. Rhianna was writing in her workbook, describing and drawing the seeds of smallflax, when he came into the kitchen.

"Hello, Father," she said, a little distracted. The shape of the seed case was tricky, and she was thinking mostly about that. Then she looked up and saw his face. "What's the matter?" she asked.

"Rhianna, we have to talk," he answered. She put down her pencil. He sat down at the table, opposite her. "Meg, come in here, will you?" he called. When Meg came in, wiping her hands, he went on, "Rhianna, this is important. We told you that you mustn't take the pendant off, except when you're getting it emptied out. Magister Northstar told you that, too. That's right, isn't it?"

Rhianna nodded.

"So," Loys went on, "why have you been taking it off?"

Rhianna stared at him, unwilling to believe he had just asked her that. "What . . . ?" she started, and stopped again. She got hold of herself with an effort. "I haven't," she said firmly. "Only in Mr. Spellwright's shop."

Loys frowned. "You're telling me that you've never taken the pendant off, all the time you've had it, except when Mr. Spellwright was emptying the magic out of it? Are you sure of that, Rhianna? Word of honor?"

Rhianna licked her lips. "Well . . . once. Once only." Her father nodded. "I took it off, for just one minute, to find out if I could use magic on the grass leaf I had drawn. And I could! I changed it into a golden bangle. But then I changed it back, put the pendant back on, and never tried again. It hasn't been off since then except in Mr. Spellwright's shop. Not at all."

Her hand had gone to hold the pendant. It felt heavy, warm with her own warmth. Her father's eyes were still narrow, not sure. He looked down, then up. "Then why are people still complaining that the magic is going missing?" he asked quietly. "They're saying that it's even worse than before. Spells are failing all over. Spells for cloth, spells for growth, spells for fishing, spells for this, that, the other thing, and everything else. The whole village has lost its magic. Why would they be saying that to me?"

Rhianna sat, stunned. "I don't know, Father," was all she managed, at last.

Loys sat back and looked at the ceiling. Rhianna suddenly thought that this was what Mr. Spellwright did: he looked over the top of her head, too. "Very well," said Loys, and his voice sounded as if it came from a distance. "I think we had better call Magister Northstar. He'll know what to do about this. I hope."

"About what, Loys? What's been going on?" Meg's voice was worried. "People have been acting oddly with me, too."

Loys ran his fingers through his hair. "What's been happening is what I said. Three times in the last two days, people have asked me what I'm going to do about that daughter of mine who's taking all the village's magic. I think Mrs. Greenapple must have been talking. Anyway, this very afternoon, Sam Farmer came in and told me that he wasn't going to pay me for that plowshare I'd made him. He said he'd take it off the bill I owed him for his ruined crop. He also told me to come to the Village Meeting. They're having one to discuss what to do about the losses caused by *my* daughter. How's that for a pleasant afternoon's work, eh?"

"It wasn't . . . they can't say . . ." Meg began.

Loys folded his arms. "They *can* say it, and they *are* saying it. We had better get Magister Northstar as soon as possible. The meeting is tomorrow afternoon. Where's that spellcaster?"

Meg got the spellcaster from the cupboard, put it on the table, and said the spell rapidly. Inside the ball of clear glass, if you looked at it the right way, there was a swirl of mist. Meg spoke the last words of the spell, *"Antheus Dexter Northstar!"* — Magister Northstar's full name.

For a second or two nothing happened, and then the mist parted and Magister Northstar's face appeared in the globe.

"Hmm?" he said, and Rhianna heard a dull clap, the sound of a book being closed. The wizard was in his study in Avalon, a hundred miles away. He peered at them and smiled. "Ah. Mrs. Wildwood. Mr. Wildwood. Rhianna. How pleasant to see you. What can I do . . ." He peered more closely. "What's the matter?" he asked sharply.

Loys told him what was happening in the village, and Magister Northstar's eyebrows drew down.

". . . and they're having a Village Meeting about it. Tomorrow afternoon," Loys finished.

In the glass, Magister Northstar's hand came into view, stroking his beard.

Meg leaned forward. "Could there be something wrong with the jewel, Magister?" she asked.

Magister Northstar pursed his lips. "It is always possible," he said, but not as though he believed it. "The magic is still going missing, you say? You're sure of that?"

Loys shrugged. "Sam Farmer told me that his crop had come in all patchy. It'll hardly be worth harvesting, he said. And the earth witch he hired to put a growing spell on it told him that there was no power in the Land to cast it. He was very annoyed."

"I see. Hmm. And Rhianna. You have not taken the pendant off, except at Mr. Spellwright's shop and that one time in the meadow at school?"

"No, Magister, I haven't."

"Could she have used so much magic doing that one change, Magister?" asked Meg.

"No, I think not. Making gold from leaves would be a fairly heavy use of magic, but Rhianna didn't make much. Just as well, and also just as well she turned it straight back."

"Why is that, Magister?" Rhianna wanted to know.

"Mmm? Oh, it's just that spell-wrought gold causes . . . difficulties. Never mind that now. Put your hand on the glass, Rhianna."

"Over your face, Magister?" asked Rhianna, startled.

"It isn't my face, Rhianna, it's just a piece of glass. Please."

Rhianna leaned forward and put her palm on the cool, round surface of the spellcaster. She could still see the edges of Magister Northstar's face around and through her fingers.

"That's right," he said. "Now. Tell me again that you did not take that pendant off, except as you have already said." Rhianna said it. He nodded. "Fine. That will do. Thank you. You can take your hand away now."

Rhianna sat back, and the globe showed Magister Northstar's face looking worried.

"I'm sure Rhianna is speaking the truth, and . . ."

At that moment his voice cut off and the globe went blank. The swirl of gray mist at its center rolled and then faded. A moment later it was just a ball of clear glass again.

"What happened?" Loys looked at his wife. "It's stopped."

Meg picked up the spellcaster, held it in her hand, frowned. "I think the spell has worn off," she said. She darted an anxious glance at her daughter. "It should have lasted longer than this."

A minute passed. Finally, Loys looked at Rhianna. Directly at her. "But it lasted long enough for Magister Northstar to say that Rhianna spoke the truth. So it's something else that's wrong. That's enough for me. I'll tell them at the meeting."

Rhianna did some figuring in her head. She hoped that Magister Northstar would think that the Village Meeting was important enough to come himself, but he was a long way away. Even the fastest ships took a day and a half to cross from Home Island. So probably the meeting would just have to take place without him. *And even if he did come,* she thought, *what could he do?*

# CHAPTER 9

The following afternoon people came to attend the meeting, which was held on the village green. They walked in, talking low among themselves, and sat down on benches and stools. Many people — forty or fifty, all from nearby. Most of them seemed worried or angry, and few were prepared to greet Rhianna or her family. Rhianna stared around her, as worried as they.

Someone sniggered behind her — Rory Spellwright. All the children were at the meeting, and so was he, thumbing his nose at her. He said something to the other children, and they laughed.

Rhianna turned away. No use getting upset about Rory. He didn't matter now.

Mrs. Fisher was the Elder this season, and at last she moved away from the knot of people she had arrived with and walked out to the front. The sun shone brightly on her face.

"All right," she said. "Quiet, please. The meeting will come to order." They stopped talking, more or less, and sat. "This is a Village Meeting. We are here to discuss the matters set out in the Bill of Calling. I'll read it to you." She unrolled a paper and squinted at it, then shaded it with her hand to see the letters. As she did so, the paper tore across with a weak, soggy noise. There was a mutter from the villagers.

"That's just the sort of thing we are complaining about," stated Sam Farmer loudly, getting to his feet. Mr. Farmer was a bulky man, red in the face — even redder now. He had a large farm up the valley, and was said to have money, too. "We don't need to read a paper to know that the magic is running out. It's become weak and unreliable. Spells are failing. But we know what the cause is, and we want to know what that family" — he turned his head and looked squarely at Rhianna and her parents — "is going to do about it."

Loys Wildwood stood up. Many pairs of eyes were fixed on him, none of them friendly. He cleared his throat. "None of us knew about Rhianna's Wild Talent," he said. "Not us, not you, not even the school." He glanced at Mrs. Greenapple. "It's very rare, I'm told. And nobody had the smallest notion that she was taking up so much of the magic of the Land, least of all her. But she isn't doing it anymore."

"No," said Mrs. Brewer, who made and sold ale. "She's left little enough to be taken."

"That isn't true. She is wearing the magic pendant that returns it all to the Land. Look!" Loys pointed.

The crowd was silent. Then a voice sounded. "She hasn't always been wearing it, though."

It was Mr. Spellwright who had spoken, and now he stood up. "Rory, my nephew, told me that. He's a truthful lad."

"He's a sneak and a coward," called Rose Treesong. People shushed her, and Mrs. Greenapple frowned at her.

Mr. Spellwright ignored the interruption. "Rory, tell the people what you told me," he said, folding his arms.

Rory could always look noble and pure-hearted when he wanted to. "I cannot tell a lie," he said. "I saw her take the pendant off to work magic. It was when she didn't think anyone could see. I bet she does it all the time."

"But *you* saw, you sneak. You're always sneaking about, looking for someone to tell on." That was Rose again, and Rhianna was grateful to her. But Rose wasn't making matters any better.

"Look, we know about that," said Loys, but he sounded weak. "She shouldn't have done it, but it was only that once. Magister Northstar said —"

Mr. Farmer cut him off. "I've heard quite enough

about that wizard. He isn't here now. We want to know what you're going to do about our losses."

"You owe me for the cost of three barrels of ale, soured and ruined," called Mrs. Brewer.

"And half my crop," added Mr. Farmer.

"And my cloth, of course. Three bolts, all useless. Fulling spell failed. You must pay for it." Mr. Natter, who made cloth, seemed to think that was obvious.

Loys shook his head. "I can't . . . we can't. We don't have that sort of money."

There was a silence. The folk looked at each other. Then Mr. Farmer clasped his hands behind his back. "If you won't pay —"

"Not won't. *Can't*," protested Meg.

"Whatever. It's your daughter's fault. You must make it good."

"It wasn't Rhianna's fault," cried Meg. "She can't help having the Talent. The school didn't —"

"Well, it isn't *our* fault," said Mrs. Greenapple loudly. "You can't blame us for it."

"I didn't say it was *anyone's* fault —" But Meg wasn't allowed to go on.

"You can't just come here and take our magic," called someone else.

"We didn't . . . we came because —"

"I lost a churn of milk just last week. All soured, gone to waste. The preserving spell failed. It's all your fault."

"Hear! Hear!" said someone else.

Voices were rising. Faces were taut and angry.

"It's cost us money!" called someone.

"Crops . . ." That was another voice.

"What about my hides? Curing spell failed . . ."

"Nets got torn across like cobwebs . . ."

"My well went dry . . ."

"Cow did just the same . . ."

"Chickens won't lay . . ." There were too many to answer, all talking at once.

"Order! Order, please." That was Mrs. Fisher. "No doubt we can all work out what we've lost and present our accounts. And then . . ."

But Mr. Farmer stepped forward. There were calls of "Move!" "Let's hear it, Sam!" and "You tell them!"

Mr. Farmer nodded. "Move, you say. So I will, then. I move, Madam Elder, that the Wildwoods pay in full for the damage their daughter has done, or . . . or" — he cast about for the worst thing he could think of — ". . . be banished. Let them forfeit their property and go back to where they came from. Yes, let them be banished. Forever. They must take their child and go and not . . . and not . . ."

And then he fell silent.

For behind him, behind them all, the sun suddenly seemed to dim, and a great blazing light sprang up. Their shadows were sharp-edged shapes before them, twisting and writhing in the flame of that hard white fire, and they swung around, everyone at the Village Meeting, all at once, as if it were a dance step. Magister Northstar had emerged onto the green from the street that ran between the houses, and they had not seen him arrive. Or perhaps he had not wanted them to see.

His staff, leaping into his hand, lit and burned with a cold light that was blinding. He rose up as tall as a mountain, his beard and eyes white flame in the light, and his robes swirled like storm clouds. They all shrank from him, Rhianna as well, for a wizard in his power is a frightening thing. And then he spoke. It was as if the Land itself spoke, slow, deep in the silence, cold and heavy in its anger. The noisy words that had gone before seemed like the squeaking of bats.

"I have heard enough," he said, and the very air shimmered and rang. "This is greed and waste. You use magic as if it were a thing to be traded and sold like a pot or a sheep, and you use it up. Farmer, how many years standing have you cropped that field, using growing spells? More than two, I'll be bound, and now you whine that your crop is poor. And you blame a child for it." He swung around so that they all were under his eye, and that eye was stony hard in judgment. "Beer and nets and hides and wells and fowls! Is there nothing you will not load on her? And all with not a voice raised to defend her, save Rose and her own parents! I tell you that this day's work is ill done, like all your work. You have much to do to make it up."

Silence. Mr. Farmer stood still, his mouth opening and closing. Magister Northstar turned to him. "You may sit," he rumbled.

Mr. Farmer wet his lips. "But . . . look here, you can't —"

"What is this you say I cannot do?" Magister Northstar gestured sharply. Mr. Farmer sat down, folding over as if broken in the middle. The wizard eyed him grimly. "I am the Mage on the Queen's Council. It is not for a Village Meeting to say what I can and cannot do. Still, for the sake of your instruction, I will answer my own question. I cannot bring the Land to harm. I cannot allow treason against the Queen. I cannot allow injustice to her subjects or wrong to a child. All the more because the child is my apprentice and under my protection. If you wrong her, you wrong me. And I say you have wronged her."

He stared at them, and this time nobody would meet his gaze. He nodded, and it was as if a mountain had moved its snowy head. "I am glad that I thought it was worth raising the wizard's wind in my sails, to come as fast as could be. For indeed, so it was. What you were about to do would have been shameful. Shameful."

Silence. Then a voice in the stillness:

"But Magister, however shall we manage if all the magic has gone away?" And Rhianna was shocked to find that the voice had been her own.

Slow time passed, a long time, it seemed, and then the Magister nodded. "Gone away, you say. Well, so it has. Let us find out where it has gone. Give me that pendant." He held out his hand.

Rhianna almost ran toward him, lifting the pendant off her neck as she came. He smiled a little, murmured a word of thanks, and took it. For a moment he let the jewel rest in his palm, and then he spoke again, while the villagers sat hushed to hear him.

"Magic is here, but not so much as to drain a district. The magic has gone somewhere else. Let us see . . ."

He handed the jewel back to her and swung his head from side to side, as if he were trying to hear where a faint sound was coming from. Then he turned and looked down the village street. "That way," he said.

Down the street he paced, following its crooked length towards the harbor. The villagers followed, carefully staying ten or twenty steps behind him as he walked, his staff clicking on the cobbles.

The houses were deserted. Everyone had gone to the meeting. The shops were closed, including the spell shop. Looking around for him, Rhianna suddenly realized that she hadn't seen Mr. Spellwright since Magister Northstar's arrival. Or Rory, either. Well, Magister Northstar had outshone everything, rather.

They passed the buildings, one by one, and Magister Northstar never paused.

At the end of the street there was a strip of green grass along the harbor wall, and then the pier jutted out as if to continue the street into the sea. Beside it rocked a single ship, tied up. Four figures stood together on the pier, their voices loud in the quiet. Magister Northstar quickened his step.

One of the figures turned. It was a man wearing a traveling cloak and hood. In his hand he carried a bag, a loaded valise that swung heavily.

Under the hood, the face was Mr. Spellwright's. He dropped the bag and it fell with a clank. His smaller companion was Rory. The other two were sailors, the crew of the vessel at the pier.

Magister Northstar's expression hardened. He swept up to the group, halted, and leaned upon his staff, three paces from them. "Well, colleague?" he asked quietly. "Going somewhere? A family outing, perhaps?"

One of the other men answered, one who wore a sailor's stocking cap. "He wanted us to take them out, right now, going anywhere, Magister. I told him you'd hired us, but . . ."

"I understand." Magister Northstar stared at the village wizard. "A sudden decision to take a sea voyage, Mr. Spellwright? I see you took some magic. Your bag is full of it, and very strong it is, too."

"I had a sudden call," blustered Mr. Spellwright. "The spells are needed."

"There's a lot of magic there for a few spells. Enough to drain a district. Perhaps I should look to make sure there isn't too much for you."

Mr. Spellwright glared. "Too much for me, you say? Why always too much for me, but not for you? It's all very well for you, with your power and your fancy robe and your wizard's staff and your college. I never went to college. Not enough power, they said. Good enough to run a stupid little shop in a stupid little village, but no better. I never had —"

Magister Northstar held up a hand. "Let me say it for you. You never had the power that you needed and wanted. But one day, it just walked into your shop. All the power you could never have. And so you took it."

Mr. Spellwright looked away, his eyes hot and resentful. Magister Northstar shook his head. "What did you use the magic for? If it was not used, it would just drain back into the earth and the stones. You could never contain so much. What did you do with it all?"

A shrug. Mr. Spellwright's face didn't change.

The staff in Magister Northstar's hand twitched. The bag shook itself, and its lock clicked. It fell open and tipped on its side.

A torrent of bright gold nuggets, smooth and rough, large and small, fell out onto the boards of the pier. Pebbles, small stones, cobbles — all had been turned into gold.

A murmur went up from the crowd.

Magister Northstar stared at the gold, and the blood drained from his face. Slowly his gaze lifted. His lips were white with anger. The sailors backed away and then broke past him into the safety of the crowd behind, leaving Mr. Spellwright and Rory to face the Magister alone. Rhianna stood behind him, watching in amazement.

"Spell-wrought gold," Magister Northstar whispered, and the whisper was as cold as the wind in winter. "You fool."

Rory began to blubber. "I told him not to!" His voice rose in a howl. "I didn't want to come! He made me!"

His uncle made a grab at him, but Rory ducked and

ran for the crowd, bawling in fear. "Made you?" shouted Mr. Spellwright. "It was you who put me up to it! 'Make some gold, like she did,' you said, 'and we can blame her.'"

But he was answered only by Rory's running feet.

People drew apart to let Rory through, holding themselves away from him as if he were dirty. He ran on, up the street, still blubbering and howling, and disappeared between the houses.

Magister Northstar had not moved. "Did you never stop to think about what you were doing, Spellwright?" he asked harshly.

"What's wrong with making a little money?" asked Mr. Spellwright. He laughed, a short bark. "Making money . . . that's what I did, all right." He laughed again.

Magister Northstar shook his head. His eyes had never left the other's face. "Do you think it's as easy as that to get rich? Did you never stop to ask why no wizard does this? Why we do not live like kings by making spell-wrought gold?"

Mr. Spellwright sneered. "Don't you live like kings, anyway? Ah, but I suppose if there was too much gold, it wouldn't be worth so much. So I only made enough for me."

But Magister Northstar had turned his back on him. He was looking up to the hills behind the village, and past them to where the mountain range reared its snowy summits into the clear sky.

"No," he said, and his voice was low and sad. "No, that's not the reason." He looked down at Rhianna. "Remember how I told you once that some things will answer if you call?" She nodded, staring up at him. "Well, making spell-wrought gold is a manner of calling, too. But it calls in a special way, and it's rather a special thing that answers."

He nodded towards the mountains. Far, far off, high in the sky beyond the peaks, there was a speck that sparkled in colors like a faceted glass in the sunlight, a speck that flew. It slowly grew to a dot, still an immense distance away, yet Rhianna knew somehow that it flew on great sweeping wings, and the light sparkled off scales that were polished like metal mirrors. As she watched, spellbound, her hand opened by itself, and her jewel, beautiful and sparkling, fell to the rough timbers of the pier. Nobody noticed.

"A dragon," said Magister Northstar. "And I am already weary."

# CHAPTER 10

"All of you, quickly." Magister Northstar was using the Wizard's Voice, the voice that stills others. "Get out of the village, out into the fields. Go as far from here as you can. The dragon isn't interested in you. Not yet, anyway. Spellwright, if you're any kind of wizard, add your magic to mine. Rhianna, go with your parents."

"Magister, my place is —"

"As my apprentice, your place is to obey me. We have no time. Go."

"Come on, Rhianna." Her father pulled her away and picked her up like a baby, his blacksmith's arms strong under her. He ran, and Meg and the others ran, too — the sailors, the villagers, all of them. Rhianna looked back over her father's shoulder at the Magister and the village wizard on the end of the pier, above the lapping sea. Magister Northstar stood, leaning on his staff; Mr. Spellwright sagged like a badly filled sack.

The villagers ran up and out of the little valley until they reached the nearest fields. There they stopped, gasping, looking down at the village and the pier and what was happening there.

"Turn the gold back to stones," Mr. Spellwright shouted. His voice broke. "The gold's what brought it, you say."

The Magister shook his head. "It would take as much magic to unmake it as it took to make it. Magic is already short because of your folly. Soon we will need all we have. And if we thwart the dragon, it will only waste the district and slaughter the people in its wrath."

His eyes never left the dragon as it slowly grew larger in the sky. It flew on vast airy wings, pulsing like a beating heart, wings of crimson shot with gold. It was not perhaps the greatest of its kind, no more than the length of the ship that rode at the pier, but it had scales like the painted shields of a hundred warriors, gold and scarlet and emerald and purple, armor that no weapon could pierce, and teeth as long as a man's arm. From its jaws rolled smoke from its living fires.

Closer it came, and closer, until it was overhead, its shadow covering pier and mages and ship, and then it began to descend. It settled, settled, and the wind from its mighty wings blew dust and wood shavings in blasts. Magister Northstar held his tall hat to his head, and

Mr. Spellwright crouched at his feet, face gray, lips moving.

The dragon landed beside the harbor wall, on the short grass before the place where the pier extended out over the sea. Dragons are creatures of air and fire, and they do not care for the great waters. Perhaps that was why the Magister had chosen to meet it there. But that was no great advantage.

It set its front hawk feet like a giant cat, and its tail, barbed and spined, trailed up the village street behind it. Its great eyes stared at the two figures at the head of the pier.

"A wizard," it said, its voice like the roaring of a huge fire. "And a hoard of spell-wrought gold. Is it your gold, wizard?"

Magister Northstar answered, his voice calm. "No. Nor anyone's."

"Then it is mine." The huge eyes flared, and a dart of flame jetted out of the open mouth.

The Magister shook his head. He looked small and slight, standing there leaning on his staff, before the jeweled length of the dragon. "Well do I know that giving gold to a dragon — spell-wrought gold above all — only strengthens it. I would not make you any stronger than you are, dragon."

The dragon hissed. It might have been dragon laughter. "What do you know of my strength, little man, little mage? It is enough that you know this: that it is far greater than yours. Stand aside, or the jewels of your robe and the ivory of your bones will be part of my hoard, too." Its head snaked forward on its long neck, and flames crackled in its nostrils.

Magister Northstar set his staff in his hand, raising it. "If your strength were as mighty as that, you would offer no bargains, dragon, and you would take as you pleased. Therefore, you have doubts. Heed them. You shall not pass. If you try to take, you shall die."

For answer the dragon breathed in, and then fire gushed from its jaws, a flood of flame. The Magister and Mr. Spellwright were caught up in it.

Mr. Spellwright yelped and scuttled in circles, crouching, his arms over his head. At the same instant the staff in Magister Northstar's hand leaped up, and the fire divided itself around them like the tongue of a snake. For a long moment the two figures were in a bubble within a sea of flame.

Yet even a dragon cannot flame forever. It pulled its head back, and the flame died.

"Quick, Spellwright," Magister Northstar called. "Join your magic to mine. You have some, at least. Boost the power of my spell."

He reached out a hand to the other man, but Mr.

Spellwright was past all reason. He knew only that he had to escape. Gibbering with fear, he ran in the only direction possible — straight at the dragon.

It reared back and hissed, and that was indeed dragon laughter. It let him pass, watching him out of its great cat eyes, and like a cat it let him think he was out of its reach. Mr. Spellwright passed the first house and dived into the space between that and the next. Then the dragon grinned and turned its head. It breathed again. Flame gushed, washing around the walls like a torrent. There was a great roaring of fire, a crackling of roof beams as they took light. Perhaps there was a terrified cry that was suddenly cut off.

Magister Northstar closed his eyes briefly. He set his feet and his staff. Still he stood between the dragon and its hoard, and the great beast turned its eyes back on him.

In that moment, Rhianna, watching from the rise above the village, wriggled out of her father's grasp and set off down the slope toward the sea, running as fast as she could. She could see what the others could not: that Magister Northstar was exhausted, and his magic was low, and there was little nearby to help him.

She heard shouts behind her, and then running feet, but they didn't matter. All around her the Land fed her its power, for the pendant still sparkled on the pier, dropped and forgotten.

Magister Northstar had taken a step back, and his shoulders were hunched, as if he were walking into driving rain. His wizard's staff still stood upright in his hand, and his other hand was tracing the rune Sophas, the rune of power, in the air.

"You shall not pass, dragon," he said again. His staff shaped the air also, and the sea grew an arm that reached out of the water. Long and thin, it whirled up, a waterspout where there was no wind, and shaped itself into a spear. The spear shimmered and whitened in the air, becoming a crystal weapon, a spear of ice. Magister Northstar gestured, and it launched itself at the dragon's heart, flashing like lightning.

The dragon had just breathed, and it had used its fire for the moment. But it was as agile as a great cat, and it leaped aside with a beat of its mighty wings. The spear flashed past, scraping a wound on its flank.

Drops of black blood rolled slowly down, but the hurt was not mortal, and the dragon reared up in its rage and its pain. It struck out blindly, and its claws were not to be batted aside like its fire. Magister Northstar was suddenly in midair, clinging to his staff as it rose like a lark into the sky. The claws passed under him, all but the tip of the uppermost; yet that was enough. The talon caught the edge of his robe, tore through and out, and the shock hurled the wizard backwards, tumbling him to the timbers of the pier. His staff fell from his grasp.

"Ha!" roared the dragon. It pulled its hindquarters under it, more like a cat than ever, to leap on him as he scrambled on hands and knees, his hat knocked off, his staff out of reach. One leap, a quick rending strike with its mighty jaws, and the fight would be over. It would take its hoard, drive out the villagers, live in the largest house, sleeping on its gold, mightier than ever before . . .

Rhianna reached the corner of the last house. She gasped, then called out —

And as the dragon's huge limbs prepared to spring, suddenly the grass it crouched on was growing over them. Hundreds, thousands of small plants, angel-eye and cow-parsley, oat grass and graywort, clover and dock and sinthel and mockweed, more than it could count, all grew in a moment, tangling and knotting themselves over its clawed feet and its barbed knees, lashing its tail to the ground, anchoring it down with millions and millions of rootlets. The dragon tore up one foot, then put it down and tore up the other, and while it did that the foot on the ground was overgrown and anchored down again.

The dragon roared, and the sound was like a mountain in the grip of an earthquake. Still Rhianna ran, gathering power as she went, power from the Land, from the sea, from the wind, from the fire. Out onto the pier she flew.

The dragon was confused, but still it had its mighty strength and its flame. It drew its head back and pulled breath in.

Rhianna had nearly reached Magister Northstar. He was on his knees and had seized his staff.

The dragon breathed out, and again the river of flame rushed down. Again the wizard's staff sprang between, and again the flame twisted and divided and roared past, hot as a furnace. But it was the Magister's last gasp. The embers of his magic flickered and died. He sank to the ground, overspent, his limbs suddenly unable to bear him up.

The spilled gold lay in a bright tumble at Rhianna's feet, and suddenly she knew what she had to do. She saw it as it was and as it must be, and she gathered the magic all around her, thin as it was, and demanded that it do her will.

The dragon tore up its huge limbs and freed itself at last. It seemed to have used up its flame, just as the Magister had used his magic, but it still had its might and its teeth and claws. It took a step towards them, and then it stopped. A hiss came from it, but this was not laughter.

For the gold it was striving for had lost its sparkle. It

dimmed and dulled, there in its careless heap on the rough timber of the pier. It took on the colors of the earth and soil again. It lost its buttery richness, its luster of metal, and became rough and common and ordinary.

Rhianna looked up. At her feet was a heap of stones.

The dragon stared. Its eyes narrowed and its head drew back. "You have taken my gold," it hissed. "Give it back."

Rhianna felt as though someone else spoke with her voice. "No, dragon," she said. Her words were calm, and seemed to come from a long way off. "I will not." She gathered up the Wild Magic, the last scraps and tatters of it, and held it as if she were drawing a bow. "It was and is a heap of stones, and a heap of stones it shall remain. Will you fight me over it, or will you go in peace?"

The dragon cocked its huge head as it considered. Then it spoke again, its voice lower than before. "There is the jewel there. It is of great price, and magical besides. Give me that and I will go. Wild as your magic is, will you measure it against mine?"

Rhianna glanced down, and there was the jewel that took away her magic, lying on the pier a pace away. Slowly, she shook her head. "No, dragon. The jewel is mine. You shall not have it. Will you fight me for it?"

It hesitated, and might have turned then. But at that moment, from around the corner between the burning houses, the villagers came running, bearing pitchforks and hatchets and scythes. At their head was Loys Wildwood, wild-eyed, his heaviest hammer whirling in a bright circle.

Rhianna could not prevent her shout: "Father! No, don't!" She stopped short.

Too late. The dragon flickered a glance at her, faster than thought. There was terrible knowledge in those eyes. Then, as fast as it had glanced, it made a grab with an armored claw, and Loys Wildwood was struggling in a grasp of steel. He struck with all his blacksmith's strength, and the heavy hammer rang off the scales and fell away, leaving a mark, a bruise. The dragon hissed in pain, but settled back on its haunches, holding its catch writhing under its clawed foot. The villagers shrank back.

"Well, now, little mage," said the roaring-fire voice. "We can bargain, you and I. *Father,* you called him, and it is said that humans value such things. Certainly he is worthier than these." The dragon's eyes dismissed the cowering villagers. "I have something you want, it seems." It nodded at the gleaming jewel on the pier. "You have something I want. Shall we trade?"

Rhianna was silent. It was her father who shouted: "No! No, Rhianna. Give it nothing. It fears you . . . ah!"

The dragon stirred. "Quiet, warrior, or I lean a little

harder and listen as you crackle." It cocked its head again. "Well, little mage? What say you?"

Rhianna looked from the jewel to her father's straining face to the dragon's slit-pupiled eyes. She nodded slowly. "Your word on your name, dragon, that he goes free unharmed and that you will depart in peace and not return, if I give you the jewel."

A groan came from her father. The dragon grinned, and lifted its huge, spike-taloned foot. "I swear it on my name," it hissed as Loys Wildwood rolled free and staggered away. "Now give me my prize."

Rhianna bent and picked up the jewel. Instantly her magic blew out like a snuffed candle. She walked toward the mighty beast, holding out the pendant in both hands.

Delicate as a duchess taking tea, it threaded the tip of a claw through the chain. It grinned again and held it up dangling from the needle point of its talon, exulting as it inspected the gleaming gold, the gems splintering the light.

But even as it did so, its eyes narrowed and became vague. The metal colors of its scales flickered and died. They became dull, first rusty, then gray-green like stagnant water. It shrank, and it became squat and uncouth in form; the long neck shortened to become a hulk of furrowed flesh. The wide wings drooped and took on the appearance of mere flaps of excess skin. It opened its mouth as if to protest, but only a lizard's hiss came out. There was no flirt of magical fire in its throat, and its eyes had become those of a beast, without understanding, dull and stupid. Its terrible grace, catlike, elegant, was gone. Stumpy legs splayed out under it. Its magic had departed. It was a great slow lizard, nothing more. The jewel had taken its magic; and dragons must have magic to be dragons.

The upraised foot it placed back on the pier, puzzled, shaking its head. What were gold and jewels to a lizard?

It was a wrong thing. Rhianna watched, knowing it would happen, and yet pitying. A dragon is a dragon, and not to be judged as if it were a thief or a bandit. She watched and knew that she could not allow this.

"Dragon," she said softly, "I will slay you if I must, but I shall not take your magic and leave you to die as a beast. It is not right."

She tugged the jewel free from under the splayed foot. Dull eyes blinked at her in bewilderment.

Holding the jewel, Rhianna walked away. As she did, color came swirling back into the dragon's scales. A dragon does not merely work magic, it *is* magic, Wild Magic in its very nature. As soon as the draining jewel was taken away, its nature returned. It grew again, long and sinuous. Its scales and claws regained their gemmed brightness and metal hardness. Its head reared up and its flashing wings filled out in enameled colors. Its limbs and body became spare and elegant and beautiful again. In its eyes grew understanding — and the understanding of its loss.

It turned its great eyes on Rhianna and hissed. Again this was dragon laughter.

But it was Rhianna who spoke. "Do you still want the jewel, dragon?" she asked.

The huge head weaved from side to side. "No, little mage. I want nothing of it."

"Then there is no more to be said. Yet I gave you the jewel, and so I hold you to the oath you swore by your name, dragon."

The dragon angled its head down to her. "You did well to spare me, and better to restore me. That is the act of a great mage." It might have meant its dip of the head as a nod of respect. "Two wizards I have defeated, but my third opponent is the mightiest of the three. I will tell my brothers and sisters this: that another Wizard of the Wild Magic has come into the world. Little mage, little mage, I think that we will meet again."

Spreading its wings with a snap that raised dust in clouds, it sprang into the air. It turned, and the great wings bore it higher, higher, faster, faster. The sun glinted off its scales as it diminished, becoming a metal eagle in the sky, then a dragonfly, a glittering wasp, a rainbow dot. To the mountains it flew, climbing above even the peaks, until it was lost, a mote in the darkening sky.

Magister Northstar pulled himself to his feet. He leaned on his staff, one hand pressed to his side. Rhianna ran to support him. Slowly and carefully they limped back towards the harbor wall together, and the villagers watched them as they came, too stunned even to cheer.

It was Loys Wildwood who scooped up the small wizard in his strong arms and carried him to where he could rest.

# CHAPTER 11

The burning houses were put out, the whole village working with buckets, hauling water from the sea. The roofless shells still smoked, their blackened window frames staring out at the harbor and at the strip of green where the dragon had sat and talked. Spots of dead grass pocked it where the dragon's blood had fallen.

Farther up the street, Magister Northstar stumbled to a bed in the inn. He lay with open, restless eyes, his hands twitching as though in a waking dream. They put his staff beside him, and Rhianna sat with him and fed him power little by little as the Land fed it to her, until his eyes closed, his breathing eased, and he slipped into natural, deep sleep. He slept the sun down and the moon down and the sun up again.

As soon as the Magister was really asleep, Loys Wildwood carried Rhianna home to her own bed. Caps were removed as he passed among the people, for the dragon had called him *warrior* and his daughter *wizard,* and those are titles of respect.

Rhianna, too, slept long. Even when she woke, late in the bright morning, the memory of weariness still seemed to soak to her very bones. Her father had gone to the smithy, making light of his scrapes and bruises, for nails and ties and strap iron would be needed to rebuild the burned houses, and he would have to make them.

Meg sang in the kitchen as her daughter emerged, tousled and still sleepy, from her room. Rhianna was eating a very late breakfast when she heard Magister Northstar's step at the door. She jumped up to give him a seat, and Meg set a bowl of porridge before him.

He thanked them and sat with a sigh, as if his knees pained him, but he ate with a good will. When he had finished, he pushed the bowl away and sat looking out of the window. Tall summer grasses were waving in the warm breeze.

"You learned your lessons well, Rhianna," he remarked. "Who'd have thought you could bind a dragon with chains made of grass?"

Rhianna shrugged. "It was all I had, Magister, and all I knew. That, and stones, and the cobbles of the street."

"It was enough to turn a dragon, and that is a very

great deal. And did you hear what he said as he departed? 'Mightiest of the three,' he called you, and it is true. Trust a dragon to know magic."

"Can you trust a dragon to speak the truth?" asked Rhianna, and the Magister smiled at the question.

"Sometimes. I think this was one of the times." He leaned back. Perhaps his beard was even whiter than it had been, the last gold gone from it now. There were more wrinkles at the corners of his eyes. When a wizard spends his power, he spends more than just his power. But his voice was firm: "You are my apprentice, and will remain so for a time, Rhianna. But the day will come when you will grow beyond me. I always knew that; now I am certain. And the dragon said one thing more. Do you remember what it was?"

Rhianna remembered. "He said that he and I would meet again."

"Yes, he said that. And perhaps that was another truth from a dragon. I don't know." He rose. "I've just come to say farewell, Rhianna, Mrs. Wildwood. I must return to Avalon. There have to be some changes made. It's well and good to use magic to heal or to calm the storm or to hold the flood or the fire, to find a lost child or to send an urgent message. But no more of this magic for everything. It will exhaust the Land. I can see that we of the

Queen's Council have done amiss to give it to every farmer and weaver and fisherman. We must confront the matter. I will go and see to it."

Rhianna nodded. Her hand came up, as if by itself, to touch the jewel at her throat. The pendant was in place again, and perhaps the village could start to get its magic back.

The Magister saw the gesture. "The College will send out a young wizard to take over Spellwright's shop. It will be, perhaps, less easy to buy magic than it has been, but a village like Smallhaven needs a wizard. He will discharge your power back into the earth again, until you have learned what you need to learn. And when you have progressed a little further in your studies, you must come to Wizardly College yourself." He looked across at Meg. "With your permission, Mrs. Wildwood, and your husband's. But I would most earnestly recommend it. In another four or five years, perhaps."

Meg nodded. Rhianna looked disappointed, though she smiled. Four or five years. A lifetime!

The Magister smiled, too. Perhaps he knew what she was thinking. "I'll look in every couple of months," he said. "I'll be watching how you grow."

The three of them walked down to the harbor together, and the folk they passed nodded and lifted their caps. At the smithy, Loys racked his tools and walked with them past the dragon-burned houses to the end of the pier, where a ship was waiting.

The wizard stepped down into the ship, the lines were cast off, and the craft heeled to the wind. He raised his staff in farewell. "Until we meet again," he called, across the widening blue water.

They waved until the ship was a white fleck of sail on the ocean. And that was the end and, in a sort of way, also the beginning.

# ABOUT THE AUTHOR

DAVE LUCKETT writes in many genres, but his first loves are fantasy and science fiction. He has won many accolades for his work, including three Aurealis Awards.

Although he was born in New South Wales, Dave has lived most of his life in Perth, Western Australia. A full-time writer, he is married with one son.

# Meet Carolyn, Maya, and Joy.

Three Girls
in the City
SELF-PORTRAIT

by Jeanne Betancourt

They couldn't be more different. But when three girls are thrown together by a summer photography class in New York City, they somehow become friends. Three girls, three cameras, one big city—find out what happens.

www.scholastic.com/books

TGCT603